D0468487

CREATIVE WOMAN MYSTERIES®

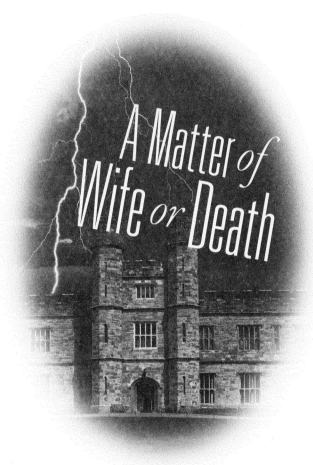
A Matter of Wife or Death

Susan Sleeman

Annie's®
AnniesFiction.com

Library of Congress-in-Publication Data
A Matter of Wife or Death / Susan Sleeman
p. cm.
I. Title
         2013914145

AnniesFiction.com
800-282-6643
Creative Woman Mysteries®
Series Editors: Ken and Janice Tate

10 11 12 13 14 | Printed in China | 9 8 7 6 5 4 3 2

— 1 —

"We're making our final descent into Glasgow, ladies and gentlemen." The cheerful flight attendant's voice crackled over the airliner's speakers. "Please remain seated, and we'll be on the ground shortly."

A burst of excitement washed the fatigue from Shannon McClain's body. Soon she would be reunited with her best friend, Coleen Douglas. She glanced at the other ladies in the Purls of Hope knitting group, who looked as excited as they had when they left the Portland airport thirteen hours earlier. Melanie Burkhart and Kate Ellis sat on either side of Shannon with Betty Russo and Joyce Buchanan across the aisle.

They'd been planning the trip for months, and each of them had something special they intended to do. Betty, a staunch Jane Austen fan, couldn't wait to walk on the same continent where the famous author had been born. As the owner of the Pink Sprinkles Bakery, Joyce planned to learn everything possible about making traditional Scottish puddings. Kate, who owned Ultimutt Grooming, hoped to see her share of purebred Scottish dogs. After her divorce, the death of her ex-husband, and her cancer survival, Melanie was ready for a new start and wanted nothing more than to bask in the joy of a traditional Scottish wedding.

"I can't believe we're almost there." Melanie's eyes were alight with wonder. "I never thought I'd be able to travel to Scotland."

"Or attend a wedding at a famous Scottish castle," Kate added dreamily. "Coleen's daughter must be so excited about such an elaborate ceremony."

Shannon thought about her friend and smiled. "Coleen's been saving for this day for years, and she's probably a whirling dervish right now."

"I was surprised she was able to take the time to pick us up at the airport." Kate turned back to the window.

"You know Coleen," Shannon said. "She likes to be part of everything."

"We're almost on the ground." Pointing out the window, Betty leaned closer to them and yawned. She was the oldest of the group, and the long travel day had taken the biggest toll on her. "Glasgow looks a lot like Oregon. Cloudy. Lush green countryside and a river—exactly like Portland."

"That's the River Clyde," Shannon said proudly. "It's the third-largest river in Scotland." A native Scot, Shannon had moved to the United States three years after her husband, John, had died in a tragic automobile accident.

Betty turned to Joyce, who was out of earshot, and repeated the conversation.

"The hills are gorgeous," Kate exclaimed as they heard the landing gear come down. "What are they called?"

"Kilpatrick Hills."

"Will we have time to hike there during the trip?"

Shannon's first scheduled stop after landing was to visit her husband's grave. Memories of her time with John took the shine off her enthusiasm. "Maybe Coleen could take you to the hills while I visit the cemetery."

"Only if you want to be alone." Melanie took Shannon's

hand. "Otherwise we'll all be at your side when you visit John."

"Of course we will," Kate added.

Melanie squeezed Shannon's hand before letting go. The wrinkle of sadness creasing Shannon's heart smoothed out at her friends' support. "You are the best friends a woman could hope for."

"Don't you know it." Melanie snapped her fingers.

With the mood lightened again, Shannon sat back in anticipation of touchdown. They hit the ground hard, the wheels bumping a few times before the tires skimmed smoothly over the runway.

"We're here!" Kate announced excitedly. She was the youngest of the Purls, and her energy seemed limitless, even after the long day.

As they rolled down the tarmac, Shannon imagined Coleen standing outside Customs, waiting to greet them. *She'll be so excited she won't be able to stand still*, Shannon thought. Oh, how Shannon missed her dearest friend. She was thrilled to be attending Gemma's wedding. Of course, Shannon didn't know if they would all survive Coleen in her super-mum mode as they helped her finish the wedding plans. The next few days would be a wild ride. Of that, Shannon was sure.

"Welcome to Glasgow," the flight attendant announced. She thanked the passengers for flying with the airline.

As soon as the plane's doors opened, Shannon clicked off her seat belt, jumped to her feet, and hurried Melanie into the aisle. Shannon wasn't used to sitting for such a long time, and it felt good to be standing.

The ladies gathered their carry-on bags, then jostled

with the crowd until all of them trudged into the terminal. Shannon started for the baggage claim area, but the others stopped to look around. Shannon gave them a few minutes to take in all the action on their first-ever trip to Scotland before hustling them through the bustling crowd to Customs.

Familiar with the procedure, Shannon entered the long queue first. She looked up at the monitor and immediately spotted Coleen waiting for them in the arrivals hall. Her bright fuchsia sweater and the quizzical tilt of her head as she looked at the arrivals board set her apart from the rest of the crowd. "Coleen's here like she promised."

Joyce raised her face to the monitor. "She can't stand still. She looks as excited as I feel."

Shannon handed her passport to the Customs agent. "I wish we didn't have to collect our luggage before talking to her."

As they made their way through Customs, Shannon kept an eye on Coleen. Coleen dug out her phone, and as she talked, Shannon saw an expression of shock come across her face. Shannon wanted to push ahead to help her friend with whatever bad news she'd obviously received. But as the hostess for the trip, she wouldn't abandon the Purls in Customs.

"I was the last one through." Betty approached Shannon, who reluctantly took her focus from the monitor.

"Let's get our luggage." Shannon hid her worry for Coleen and led her friends to the baggage claim area.

After another fifteen minutes, they emerged in the arrivals hall with bags in tow. Coleen came running forward. She smiled, but Shannon could tell she had forced herself to put on a cheery face for them.

"Och! Look at the five of you on Scottish soil!" she

exclaimed. "I'm so thrilled to welcome all of you." She drew Shannon into a fierce hug.

"You got bad news on your phone call," Shannon whispered. "Do you want to talk about it?"

"And spoil this reunion?" She tightened her arms around Shannon.

Shannon drew back and appraised her friend. "Are you sure?"

She nodded vigorously. "Now kindly step aside, dear friend, so I can properly welcome the others."

Coleen pulled Joyce into a hug first. "The sweet scent of sugar and baked goods lingers on you as usual. I hope you brought me one of your famous cupcakes."

Joyce lifted her carry-on bag. "You'll find six of them in here just for you. I had to tell Customs they're for my personal consumption. Don't rat me out!"

Coleen rubbed her tummy. "You're too good to be true."

"Me next." Kate slipped between them.

Coleen ran her gaze over Kate. "Well now, my bairn. Don't you look fetching in your frilly little top?"

"I wanted to dress up for the trip, so Melanie took me shopping in Portland." Usually dressed in a T-shirt boasting a crazy animal slogan, Kate blushed under Coleen's praise as she hugged her.

Shannon nudged Melanie. "You did an amazing job of choosing her blouse. She does look wonderful in that shade of green."

Coleen released Kate and held her arms out to Melanie. "Still getting good reports from the doctor, I hope?"

"Cancer free." Tears welled up in Melanie's eyes, but Shannon knew they weren't tears of sadness, but joy of being in remission from her recent breast-cancer scare.

"Hey, come over here and hug me so we can explore this beautiful country," Betty said in her no-nonsense tone. "We can catch up in the car."

"I see you're still the practical one of the group." Coleen slipped her arms around Betty.

When they broke apart, Shannon noted the worried expression had returned to Coleen's face, though she quickly wiped it away. "I rented a minivan, so follow me."

Coleen bustled off in her usual bull-in-the-china-shop approach to life, and the Purls scurried to keep up with her.

Outside, a chilly wind hit Shannon in the face, and she wished her hands were free from luggage to button her coat. "Colder than usual, huh?"

"Aye," Coleen said. "We've been having a cold snap."

"Before we take another step, I need everyone to gather by that sign for a picture." Melanie pointed at an airport sign and pulled out her camera.

When the Purls had assembled in an orderly group, Melanie stopped a pleasant-looking woman who agreed to snap their picture.

Joyce's teeth chattered as she passed Shannon, so she snuggled the group closer together. "Wouldn't do for our first picture here to look like we're not having a good time."

Photo complete, Melanie clapped her hands. "OK, our adventure in Scotland can now begin."

"Way to take charge, Melanie," Coleen said over her shoulder as she headed for the parking lot.

Melanie caught up to Coleen. "I don't want you to think I'm being pushy. The Purls appointed me as the official group photographer." She grinned at Coleen. "We have a weekend scrapbooking retreat planned. If I don't do a good job, they're sure to lynch me."

"I doubt they'd actually hang you. They're into crafts, so tarring and feathering you is more their style." Coleen's lighthearted laugh reverberated around the multistory parking garage. She unlocked a bright red minivan. Shannon smiled over the color choice, which was so fitting with Coleen's audacious personality.

The lift gate swung up, and Shannon helped load the luggage. "You'll have a hard time seeing over this pile."

"I'll manage." Coleen slammed the gate, the sound echoing through the structure.

Shannon wrinkled her nose at her friend. "That's what I'm afraid of. Your driving is already sketchy."

Shannon expected Coleen to protest. Instead, she pulled Shannon into a bear hug. "How I've missed you. I'm so happy you're here."

Tears of happiness threatened to spill over, so Shannon pushed back and forced a lighthearted tone to her voice. "Who wants to sit in front?"

"You should," Joyce answered. "You haven't been home in months, and we know you'll want to take it all in."

"Agreed." Coleen hurried to the driver's side of the vehicle. Shannon paused for a moment. She'd been in America long enough that seeing her friend rush to the right side of the car felt odd.

The Purls piled into the van. Kate and Melanie took seats in the rear, Joyce and Betty in the center row. As Shannon slid the side door open, she caught sight of Kate, who'd scrunched her eyes closed.

Baffled, Shannon asked, "Are you OK, Kate?"

She shook her head. "Driving on the wrong side of the road has me freaked out. I don't think I can watch."

Melanie slipped her arm into Kate's. "You have to at least try it, or you'll miss all the sights."

"We don't call it the 'wrong side' here," Coleen said. "You may drive on the right side of the road in the States, but we drive on the 'proper' side." The Purls joined in a chuckle with their Scottish friend.

"I'll try," Kate said, nodding, but she still looked skeptical. Shannon closed their door and settled in the front seat. Coleen shifted into gear, and they soon exited the airport and merged onto the motorway leading to Wainscot. Thick Monday-morning traffic clogged the road, but Shannon was too busy taking in the familiar scenery to care.

"This is too weird," Kate said, drawing Shannon's attention. "I don't know how you ever got used to driving in Oregon."

"How long is the drive?" Melanie pressed her face against the window.

"Och, with this traffic, forty-five minutes at least," Coleen replied.

"Great. That'll give us time to get a feeling for the countryside." Melanie aimed her camera out the window. "I'm so thrilled at all the things we get to do on this trip that I've never done before. An international flight, a trip on a ferryboat, a Scottish castle. These are things I've only dreamed of before."

"I aim to make your dreams come true," Coleen replied, but her ringing phone quickly distracted her.

Fearing Coleen couldn't keep track of an incoming call, the conversation, and the wheel at the same time, Shannon picked up her friend's phone. Gemma's name flashed on the screen. "It's Gemma. Do you want me to answer?"

"Please," Coleen replied.

Shannon pressed the icon. "Hello, Gemma. It's Shannon."

"Mum!" the girl screamed. "I need Mum."

"She's driving. I'll put you on speaker." Shannon turned to Coleen. "She's upset about something."

Coleen *tsked*. "She's been in a tizzy with all the wedding details."

Shannon didn't doubt that, but Gemma's tone was extreme, even for a bridezilla. "Go ahead, Gemma. You're on speaker."

"They're here, Mum. At the castle. Waiting for you." Her words tripped over each other.

"Now slow down, honey," Coleen said in an unusually calm tone for her. "Who's there?"

"The police, of course. They think you're involved in the murder."

Gasps of surprise emanated from the backseat, and Shannon shot a look at Coleen. "What murder?"

"Did I forget to mention it?" Coleen said innocently.

"Don't toy with me, Coleen Douglas. You know you did."

"Our wedding planner, Siobhan Paterson, was murdered in her office on the castle grounds."

"And why are the police waiting for you?"

"Mum had a big argument with Siobhan." Gemma's frustration with her mother flowed from the phone. "A real knock-down, drag-out fight, if you must know."

Shannon eyed Coleen. "Is that true?"

"She was embezzling from her clients." Coleen clenched her fist. "What kind of woman takes advantage of a man and woman on the most important day of their lives?"

"We don't know that she's stolen from me, Mum," Gemma said. "You put the cart before the horse as usual and accused her without any proof."

Shannon heard a loud male voice in the background and wondered if it was a police officer.

"I've gotta go," Gemma said. "Please hurry, Mum. I can't deal with this right now."

"I'll be there as soon as I can, honey."

Shannon disconnected and faced Coleen. "Turn the car around and head straight for the ferry."

"But the cemetery …."

"There'll be time after the wedding to visit." Shannon patted Coleen's knee. "Gemma needs you now."

"Are you sure?"

"Of course I'm sure." Shannon pivoted toward the Purls. "You don't mind heading straight for the castle, do you?"

"Are you kidding?" Melanie said. "Who would mind going straight to an exciting Scottish castle?"

"Not me." The silvery earrings Shannon had made for Joyce's birthday swung below her platinum bob.

"Agreed," Betty said.

"I'm in." Kate pulled her focus from the road, looking a bit queasy.

Shannon watched as Kate blinked rapidly for a moment. "Are you OK, sweetie?"

"I'm feeling nauseous."

Betty turned to Kate. "Do you get carsick?"

"Not usually, but maybe I was focusing too hard on the road." She laid her head back on the headrest. "I'll close my eyes for the rest of the ride."

"Poor thing." Betty reached over the seat and took Kate's hand. "Take a rest. We'll be at the ferry before you know it."

"Then the castle," Melanie said dreamily.

And the police, Shannon thought, and Coleen's face said she was thinking the same thing. Shannon hoped that by the time they arrived, the police would have located the person who killed Siobhan, allowing Coleen to focus on her daughter's wedding. If not, Shannon would offer her services as amateur sleuth. Despite the jet lag that was threatening to lull her to sleep, she'd dig in and locate the killer.

2

Phone to ear, Shannon waited for the CalMac Ferry reservation agent to take her off hold. Hamilton Castle sat on the Isle of Arran, and the best way to reach it from the mainland was by a large ferry that would carry their van. Since they had originally planned to visit John's grave first, Coleen had scheduled them to depart Ardrossan on a later ferry. Now Shannon had to make sure the earlier boat had room.

After another five minutes, the agent came back on the line and confirmed their reservation. Shannon disconnected her phone. "We're good to go with the earlier one."

Betty shook her head. "I never imagined you'd need reservations to board a ferry."

"Not all ferries require it, but this route is a busy one." Coleen piloted the minivan around a circle in the road and exited onto the harbor drive that would take them to the dock. "That's the last roundabout."

Joyce craned her neck to see out the front window. "I never thought we'd see so many traffic circles."

"Get used to them," Coleen said sardonically. "We're famous for going in circles around here."

"Speak for yourself." Shannon clutched her chest in mock offense.

The ladies laughed, and when their laughter died down, the car fell silent. Shannon studied her fellow travelers. They'd all succumbed to weariness on the drive, and

Shannon wouldn't be surprised if they headed straight to bed once they arrived at Hamilton Castle despite their desire not to waste a minute of their trip. Indeed, Shannon herself would have loved to drop into bed, but Coleen needed her.

When the large white ferry came into view, excitement over attending Gemma's wedding made Shannon reach out and squeeze Coleen's hand.

Coleen cast a quizzical look at her. "What was that for?"

"Despite all our phone conversations, it just hit me. Our little Gemma's getting married." Shannon had known Gemma and her sister, Olivia, for so long that she thought of them as part of her own family.

Coleen's eyes turned impish. "And as her adopted mum, I hope you'll be sharing in the cost of the wedding."

Shannon swatted at Coleen, who fixed her attention on steering their van into the four-lane queue waiting to board the ferry.

Kate lowered her window and stuck her head out. "Wow. I didn't think the boat would be *this* big."

"Good thing it is, or our van wouldn't fit," Melanie teased.

Shannon laughed. "If they haven't changed boats since I lived here, this ferry can hold sixty-some cars and over six hundred people. Plus there's a cafeteria, coffee shop, game room, and a gift shop."

"Wow." Melanie shook her head in amazement. "Just wow."

Coleen's stomach grumbled. "The boat ride is about an hour long, which is plenty of time to grab breakfast in the cafeteria."

Kate raised the window. "Can we sit outside?"

Shannon glanced at the dash. "The thermometer says it's only thirty degrees outside, and that's without the wind, which I can guarantee will be blustery this time of year."

"Right you are." Coleen pretended to shiver. "I'm a rugged Scot, and even I won't sit outside in these temps."

"Still, I'm up for it." Kate's cheeks had turned pink from hanging her head out the window. No telling how red they'd be after an hour on deck. "Who's with me?"

"I'll join you for a little while, but these old joints don't much like cold anymore." Betty rubbed her knees.

"I don't know," Joyce said through a long yawn.

Betty nudged her. "Come on. It will wake you up."

"Look. Cars are coming out." Melanie pointed at the front end of the boat, which had opened wide, resembling a whale's mouth.

They watched as cars and trucks disembarked, and when the deckhand flagged them ahead, Coleen eased the van into the belly of the boat. The tires rumbled over the metal ramp extending from the front of the boat onto the dock. They followed a yellow line into the two-story hull until another deckhand signaled for Coleen to stop.

"This is so cool." Melanie popped the lens cap off her camera.

"I feel another group picture coming on, and I'm going to be ready for this one." Joyce dug lipstick out of her purse.

"You are so right." Melanie laughed. "The sign by the steps is perfect, and then we'll take another on deck."

Shannon grabbed her purse and climbed from the van. She shivered and dug gloves from her pocket. They lined up by the sign, and Melanie once again stopped a woman to take the photo.

"This way," Coleen said as she started for the stairs.

Shannon linked her arm in Coleen's. "Let's head up to Deck 4, where the hardy bunch can sit outside and you and I can sit in the cafeteria."

They climbed the stairs to Deck 4, where the wind slapped Shannon's hair into her face. She tugged her coat closed. "Let's hurry up with this picture."

"I agree." Coleen moved the group into position and, instead of waiting for Melanie to find a photographer, Coleen grabbed an employee. The waves hitting the boat's hull sent them knocking into each other.

"This is such fun," Kate exclaimed when they'd moved out of their formation. She rushed to the edge of the railing and started snapping pictures with her cellphone.

Melanie crossed the deck and tripped over a bench. She giggled like a little child. "I feel like a drunken sailor."

Shannon loved seeing Scotland through the eyes of newcomers. Every event, no matter how mundane, was fresh and exciting to them.

Coleen tucked her hair behind her ear, but the wind freed it instantly. "Let's get out of the wind before we hit the open waters where the wind gusts pick up."

"Don't wait until you're frozen solid to join us." On unsteady legs, Shannon followed Coleen inside and rubbed her chilly hands together. "A cup of tea would be lovely right now."

"Sit, and I'll get it." Coleen held her hand toward an open table large enough for the entire group.

Shannon didn't argue but took a seat facing the window and let the warm air flow over her chilled body. She watched the Purls huddled at the rail. Though they appeared cold, when the ferry horn blew and they set sail, their faces grew animated. If Shannon hadn't wanted a moment alone with Coleen to talk about the wedding planner's murder, she'd have joined in the fun.

Coleen returned carrying a tray with steaming cups of tea. "Ah, it does my heart good to see you and all the Purls on Scottish soil."

"Feels good to be back for a visit."

Coleen cocked a perfectly plucked eyebrow as she sat. "You wouldn't want to move back now, would you?"

Shannon shook her head. "Sorry. I'm enjoying the craft market and my life in Oregon too much."

"I had to ask." Coleen stared over the choppy waves and yawned. "I'm as tired as the lot of you. Too many nights spent on the wedding."

Shannon's hands wrapped around her teacup, the warmth taking away the last of her chill. "I'm so glad you asked all of us to help bead Gemma's gown. I can't wait to get my hands on it."

"Practice for when Lara gets married."

At the thought of her daughter getting married, Shannon shuddered. "Don't even talk that way. As a college sophomore, she's way too young to marry." Lara and her twin brother, Alec, had followed Shannon to the States and were students at Portland State University.

Coleen winked over her cup. "I know, I know. I was having a bit of fun with you."

Shannon rolled her eyes at her friend, then glanced outside to see how the Purls were faring now that the ferry was cresting large waves. They still huddled together at the rail, but they held on. As the ferry hit a wave, they slid side-ways in unison and laughed. Shannon didn't want a thing to spoil their trip, and the death of the wedding planner had potential to do so. She had to make sure her friends still had a wonderful time.

"Since we're alone for a bit, why don't you tell me about this murder," she said to Coleen, hoping to get the facts before the others came inside.

Coleen's forehead furrowed. "Do we have to talk about it?"

"If I know all the details, I might be able to help you when we get to the castle." Shannon took a long drink of her tea.

Coleen sighed. "There's not a lot to tell."

"How about starting with why you thought Siobhan was embezzling."

"Hamilton Castle has a lovely caretaker couple, Greer and Fiona Burke. I was passing by their office and over-heard them talking about Siobhan. They didn't know I was listening, so they spoke freely about a bride who'd called demanding to speak to Siobhan. She was out of the office, so the bride told Fiona that Siobhan stole money from her account. She claimed Siobhan had padded the bills, then pocketed the difference."

"Did she have any proof?"

"She said she did, but I couldn't very well ask for it without telling them I was eavesdropping."

"Gemma is right. You talked to Siobhan prematurely."

Coleen's face fell. "I guess so, but we need every penny I scrimped and saved to pull off this wedding. I couldn't risk Siobhan taking even one cent."

"I would probably have done the same thing." Shannon

took Coleen's hand. "As would most mothers of the bride."

"Apparently I was the only one who talked to her, though. Siobhan claimed innocence and said no one else had contacted her."

"Maybe the bride who phoned was the only person who discovered it. Or maybe Siobhan only stole from that bride. Or maybe the bride had an axe to grind over something else and made the whole story up. Did you get her name?"

"No, but Fiona should know it."

"If the police still suspect you after your interview, I'll talk to her." Shannon patted Coleen's hand, then picked up her cup again.

A pensive look stole across Coleen's face, and for a moment, she stared into the distance. "I hate that this is putting a damper on your trip—not to mention Gemma's wedding—but I'm thankful to have you here. Will you stay with me while the police question me?"

"If they'll let me. We're not in Apple Grove, where Chief Grayson knows me." Shannon pondered the scene that would be waiting for them at the castle. "Of course, the castle is in a rural area, so maybe we'll be dealing with a local constable who might bend the rules a bit."

"Let's hope so." Coleen nodded at the window. "They've finally had enough."

Still laughing, the Purls tromped inside. Betty rubbed her arms. "All that fresh air has made me hungry."

Coleen looked at her watch and stood. "If we hurry, we can enjoy a traditional Scottish breakfast."

"I'm game for that." Shannon got up and headed for the food line, where the worker loaded her plate with bacon, eggs, a potato scone, black pudding, onion, and a tomato as Shannon described the items to the girls.

Kate narrowed her eyes. "The pudding is made from pig's blood?"

"It's good," Coleen said.

Kate shook her head. "I'll try it so I can say I did, but I'm not holding out hope that it will actually be good."

With all their trays filled, they returned to the table and tucked into the food. Kate didn't like the black pudding, but Betty, Joyce, and Melanie did. As they talked about other Scottish delicacies like haggis, which is made in a sheep's stomach, Kate turned a little green. Shannon didn't know if it was from the food, the waves, or the conversation.

As the ferry neared the Isle of Arran, they all traipsed outside to observe the docking. Memories of Shannon's first ferry ride as a child with her father flashed into her head, and she guessed the wonder on her face matched the Purls' expressions.

"Why aren't the other passengers watching?" Melanie asked as she snapped pictures.

"People who live on the island make this trip all the time," Coleen explained. "They're more interested in getting into their cars and on with their business than watching the boat dock."

"We don't often appreciate the wonders in our own backyard." Shannon draped an arm around Melanie. "But I love seeing it through your eyes. I'd like it more if it wasn't so darn cold."

Shannon and Melanie stayed close together for warmth until the boat docked, then made their way down to the vehicle. Once everyone was back in the same seating arrangement, Coleen inched the van forward.

"Is it normal for the police to be here?" Melanie asked.

"Not normal, but not unheard of," Coleen answered. "People have been known to try to elude the police by fleeing to the islands."

Shannon craned her neck and spotted two male police officers dressed in traditional uniforms standing next to a deckhand. They peered into every car and stopped a few to talk to the drivers. Unease churned the breakfast in Shannon's stomach, but Coleen appeared unconcerned as she moved the van up to the police officers. The tallest one looked in the window and suddenly flipped up his hand.

"Wouldn't you know I'd be the one he stopped?" Coleen abruptly put on the brakes and powered down her window.

"Are you Coleen Douglas?" he asked gruffly, and Shannon's heart sank.

"I am," Coleen replied.

"I'm afraid you'll have to come with us, ma'am."

"I don't understand," Coleen said. "What's this all about?"

He shrugged. "All I know is I've been asked to meet your ferry and escort you to Hamilton Castle." He jabbed a finger at the parking lot. "You can park over there. Your friends are welcome to drive your vehicle, but you'll be riding with us."

Coleen's mouth dropped open, and her gaze flew to Shannon.

Shannon didn't know what to say. In her long friendship with Coleen, Shannon had never seen Coleen at a loss for words. And with the desperate cry for help on Coleen's face, Shannon hoped never to see Coleen speechless again.

3

Coleen parked the van and sat staring at the wheel. Not surprising. Shannon would be in shock too if a police officer met her at the ferry and insisted she accompany them. But shock might make Coleen say or do something during the interrogation that could have further repercussions.

Shannon turned to the Purls. "Is anyone comfortable driving the van so I can ride along with Coleen?"

"I'm game," Joyce answered. "As long as you give me directions and someone navigates."

Shannon caught Coleen's attention. "I'll talk to the officers. I'm sure they'll let me ride with you."

Coleen nodded but didn't speak.

Shannon jumped out of the van and approached the officers, who stood near their vehicle. The tall officer's badge identified his last name as MacGregor, and he tapped his foot impatiently.

Shannon decided to start with the more relaxed one. She read "Brodie" on his name tag. "Would you mind if I rode with Coleen?"

He appraised her. "I can't see any reason why you would need to do so."

"She's shaken up, and it would make the ride easier for her and you if I held her hand."

Brodie cocked an eyebrow. "Easier for us?"

Shannon nodded sincerely. "Coleen likes to jabber when

she's upset. She'll talk your ear off all the way to the castle."

Brodie watched Shannon for a few moments, then tossed a questioning look at MacGregor, who shrugged.

"Fine," Brodie said. "But see that you don't cause any trouble."

Shannon hurried back to the van and opened Coleen's door. "I have permission to ride with you."

Coleen smiled weakly. "Good."

"Joyce will need directions to the castle in case we get separated."

"It's easy to find." Coleen dug out a folder next to her seat and withdrew a map that she handed to Joyce.

Joyce looked it over. "We shouldn't have any problems."

Shannon smiled her thanks at Joyce. "I'm sure the police will take us straight to the door, so we'll see you inside the castle."

Coleen stepped out of the van and, with a deep breath, raised her shoulders. Color returned to her face, and Shannon knew the feisty Coleen was trying to make a comeback. With any luck, she'd be her spirited old self by the time they arrived at the castle.

To the chorus of best wishes from the Purls, they marched to the police car. Brodie opened the back door, and Coleen slid in first. Shannon had never ridden in a police car in Scotland, and she let the gadgets in the front distract her until Coleen drew her closer.

"Do you think they believe I killed Siobhan?" she whispered.

"Not likely."

"Then why do you think they're escorting me to the castle?"

Shannon hadn't had time to think about why the police had come for Coleen, so she gave it some consideration before answering. "The only reason I can think of is they didn't believe Gemma when she said you were on your way."

"But that shouldn't matter if they don't suspect me."

"True," Shannon admitted reluctantly. "But it's a waste of time to worry about this."

"Easy for you to say."

"Hey," Shannon said a bit too loudly, catching Brodie's attention. She lowered her voice. "C'mon. Where's the spunky Coleen we all know and love?"

"I left her on the boat."

Shannon giggled. "That's my girl."

Coleen took in a deep breath. "Promise me something."

"Of course."

"If the police somehow think I'm involved in the murder, and I let it get to me, tell me to knock it off. I don't want to ruin the week for Gemma or the Purls."

"Let me get this straight." Shannon paused and stared at Coleen. "You—Coleen Douglas, my dearest friend who's known for her wild and crazy stunts—are giving me permission to call you out?"

"Maybe not on *all* my actions. Just the ones related to Siobhan." A devilish grin claimed Coleen's mouth. "Let's use this time to figure out what I'm going to do without a wedding planner."

"I don't suppose you could find someone else at such short notice?"

"Not likely, especially with me under investigation for

the murder of my last wedding planner. And definitely not someone who knows Hamilton Castle like Siobhan did. With castle weddings so popular, the owners gave her room and board plus paid her wages to work exclusively for castle guests."

"Might the caretakers you mentioned know anything about the plans?"

Coleen shrugged. "They should at least know about the facility use, but there are so many details I know nothing about. I don't even know who's scheduled to officiate at the ceremony."

"There can't be too many ministers in the area."

"But what if Siobhan usually brings in someone from the city?"

"I'm guessing the caretakers would know the answer to that as well."

"I need to make a list of all the questions so when we're done with the police, I can talk to Fiona." Coleen lifted her purse and dug out a notepad and pen. She tapped her chin, then started scribbling notes on the paper.

Shannon directed her attention to the countryside. Ominous clouds rushed to darken the skies and fat raindrops plopped onto the windshield. The rhythm of the rain lulled Shannon into a drowsy state, and she felt her eyelids drop. She blinked hard, but despite Herculean efforts, it was difficult to keep her eyes open, and she succumbed to sleep.

"Shannon." Coleen's voice broke into Shannon's dream. "We're almost there."

Shannon climbed out of the sleep tunnel and blinked

hard. She yawned and stretched.

"Sorry to wake you," Coleen said. "I know how tired you must be."

"I'm glad you did." Shannon arched her neck to get a good view of the grounds through the metal screen. "I haven't been here in years, and I wanted to see the castle when we arrived."

They rounded the curve and the sun broke free, shining down on the magnificent castle. Shannon's breath caught as she took in the six tall turrets with pointed green roofs stretching toward the sky. The ruddy stone almost seemed to glow with the vibrant history of the building. A rich, manicured lawn surrounded the front side of the estate, but Shannon knew from her previous visits as a child that the backside abutted the waters of Loch Hamilton, a sheltered sea loch. Several traditional cottages housing the staff were nestled at the rear of the property as well, and a formal garden took up most of one side.

Shannon clutched Coleen's hand. "I forgot how lovely this is."

"Aye. It's one of the most beautiful estates in our fair land."

"And you've worked so hard to make sure your equally beautiful daughter has the wedding that dreams are made of." Shannon sighed. "I hope she appreciates all you've sacrificed for her."

"At twenty-four, I doubt she can fully appreciate it, but she will in time." Coleen's lips broke into a wistful smile. "Imagine the pictures we'll have."

As the visions peppered Shannon's brain, the car wound down the long drive. Two police cars and a van belonging to the Police Casualty Surgeon—Scotland's version of a medical examiner or coroner—sat silently near the massive double-door entrance. Shannon tried to hold on to the sweetness of their arrival, but when Coleen tightened her grasp, it floated away.

"You'll stay with me?" Coleen asked as the car came to a stop and the officers got out.

"Of course I will." Shannon leaned closer and whispered, "Keep your answers short and to the point. No rambling, or you might say something you'll regret."

"Me? Ramble?" Coleen mocked offense, then broke into a boisterous laugh that Shannon thought was fueled by stress.

"This will all be fine," Shannon said. "You have the power of the Purls behind you now, and we won't let a thing go wrong."

"Aye, I know you won't." Coleen quickly hugged Shannon, then climbed out. She drew her shoulders into a straight line and looked Officer MacGregor in the eye. "Take me to your leader."

Shannon chuckled at her friend's humor as she scrambled from the car. She saw the Purls' van stop at the road and wished she could be with them as they discovered this magnificent piece of Scottish history.

"Best not keep Watson waiting." MacGregor jerked his head toward the thick wooden door.

Shannon tried to focus on Coleen's predicament, but it was hard to do with the solid stone building begging for exploration. The aged door groaned open as if tired from years of use. How many people had stepped over the centuries-old threshold? What were their stories—and would Shannon learn about them as she explored the interior?

They stepped into a large hall, and Shannon turned in a circle to take in the massive space. A wide wooden staircase boasting an ornately carved banister led to an alcove with stained glass windows. Polished wood with thick moldings adorned the walls, and tapestry rugs covered tiled floors.

A short, stumpy man in a rumpled beige raincoat clomped across the room. A redhead, his fair skin was mottled with freckles, and his cheeks were wind-kissed. His smile was pleasant as he withdrew a badge, and Shannon was happy to see that the officer who would question Coleen appeared to possess a pleasant demeanor.

"Mrs. Douglas, I presume?" he asked, holding up his badge and then putting it back in his pocket.

Coleen nodded.

He shifted a notebook to his left hand and stuck out the other. "Detective Inspector Declan Watson."

Coleen clasped the man's fingers, but Watson's gaze had already traveled to Shannon. He let his gaze rove up and down quickly, then he eyed MacGregor. His eyes were sharp and appraising, taking away Shannon's earlier impression.

"This is my friend, Shannon McClain, from the United States," Coleen offered.

Watson kept his focus on MacGregor, who took a step back. "We thought it harmless to let her friend ride along."

Watson shook off his intensity, his smile returning as he

held out his hand. "Welcome to Scotland, Ms. McClain."

Shannon nearly winced at the man's firm grasp. "Thank you."

Watson's eyes widened at her brogue. "You're one of us?"

"Aye," Shannon said. "Born and raised. I just recently relocated to Oregon. Do we call you Detective or Inspector?"

He waved a hand. "Doesn't matter to me. Either will do, or simply call me Watson."

Just like Chief Grayson back in Apple Grove prefers to be called Grayson, Shannon thought. She did not want to get personal with the man who was going to interrogate Coleen. "Inspector should be fine."

He'd opened his mouth to speak when the door swung open, grabbing his attention. Chattering excitedly, the Purls entered the room but fell silent as they took in the foyer with openmouthed wonder.

"Oh, Coleen, it's fabulous." Betty spun in a circle as Shannon had done.

"Thank you for inviting us," Kate cried out.

Melanie started snapping pictures, including one of Inspector Watson.

He held out his hand, warning her to back off. "More friends from America?"

Coleen nodded.

"Perhaps we should move to the library for privacy," he suggested.

Coleen shook her head. "They've had such a long trip. I'd like to find the caretakers so my friends can settle into their rooms and then check in with my daughter."

"MacGregor!" Watson barked. "Fetch the butler and see that the Americans are taken care of."

"But—" he said, then halted when Watson flashed a fiery gaze at him. "Right away, sir."

As MacGregor rushed off, Shannon was beginning to see that Watson wasn't the unassuming man she'd first thought, and she wondered how he would treat Coleen. Would she get the convivial gentleman they'd first encountered or the demanding inspector?

"Thank you for your help," Coleen said. "I'll run up to my daughter's room and be right back."

Watson's smile faltered. "I'm afraid that will have to wait, Mrs. Douglas."

"But she's so worried," Coleen explained. "She's getting married on Saturday, you see, and we have so many things to do. The beading on her dress isn't finished. We don't have a clue what's happening with the minister, and then there are the other arrangements that Siobhan alone knew about. I can't waste a moment with all of this outstanding." Coleen paused to draw in a deep breath.

"Our talk won't take long." An unyielding expression consumed his face as he gestured to a room, clearly meaning Coleen had better comply. "The library is right this way."

Shannon held up a hand. "I'd like to join you for the questioning."

One of his thick eyebrows shot up again. "This isn't an interrogation. Just a pleasant little chat."

"If it's only a little chat, then I'm sure you won't mind if I sit in." Shannon didn't wait for his approval but linked arms with Coleen and turned toward her friends. "We'll be in the library with the inspector. The butler is on his way to show you to your rooms. We'll come find you when we're free."

"Good luck, Coleen," Joyce called out, and the others murmured their support.

Shannon felt Coleen slump, undoubtedly worried. "Shoulders back, head high," she whispered to Coleen. "We're two tough women, and we can take on one inspector."

Coleen winked. "He won't know what hit him."

They wound through gleaming antique furniture and under a high doorway. Red flocked wallpaper covered the library's walls, which were ringed with ornate bookshelves, the highest ones accessible by means of a rolling ladder. A crackling fire burned in the fireplace under an oil painting of a stern male ancestor in a gilded frame, his expression as sour as Watson's had turned.

Shannon led Coleen to a green velvet sofa under a wall of smaller paintings and sat. Watson chose a mahogany cane-backed chair and perched on the edge. He laid his notebook on his lap. As he opened his mouth to speak, the sun gleaming through the tall windows disappeared, casting the room in a gloomy pall.

Shannon waited for the first question and hoped the sun's disappearance hadn't foretold the outcome of their meeting.

— 4 —

Watson wasted no time but placed his focus squarely on Coleen. "Let's start with you telling me when and where you met with Ms. Paterson Sunday."

He sounded relaxed, but Shannon knew he was simply trying to get Coleen to let her guard down. Shannon glanced at her friend and tried to warn her with a pointed look.

Coleen blinked her acknowledgement. "Right after dinner. Around eight, I guess. In her office."

Watson's head tilted in interest. "And how did the meeting go?"

"As I'm sure you've heard by now, I confronted Siobhan about her embezzlement, and our meeting escalated into an argument." Coleen recounted the same story she'd told Shannon on the ferry. "I'd recently transferred a large sum of money to Siobhan to pay expenses. The Burkes said she had padded bills and pocketed the difference. I asked to see our invoices again so I could review them."

"And did she produce them?"

"Yes, and they all looked to be in order." Coleen took a deep breath. "Not that I could verify it at the time, mind you. With the bills in hand, I planned to phone our vendors directly to confirm the amounts."

"So you don't possess actual *proof* that Ms. Paterson embezzled money from your account?"

"Correct. I simply wanted to get copies of all the

invoices and tell her I knew about her illegal activities so she'd leave our money alone." Coleen smiled. "I'm confident that with your investigative skills you'll find all the proof you need of embezzlement."

Shannon felt like gagging at Coleen's obvious attempt to butter up Watson.

He didn't seem to care if the compliment was genuine as he puffed out his chest. "You do realize if I find such proof, it will cement you on my suspect list."

Coleen swallowed hard. "But why? She may not have taken money from us."

"Still, you thought she might have when you confronted her. That gives you a motive to want to harm her."

"But I didn't." Coleen shot a worried look at Shannon.

"If Siobhan is indeed guilty of embezzlement, there must be other brides or mothers of the bride who might've wanted to harm her," Shannon said.

"We'll get through this faster if you keep your interruptions to a minimum." Watson burned Shannon with a withering look.

"I was only trying to point out that there are likely many other suspects to investigate."

"Yes, but Mrs. Douglas is the only one who met with Ms. Paterson last night. And ..." He changed his focus to Coleen, and Shannon knew bad news was forthcoming. "At this point, we believe you, Mrs. Douglas, were the last person to see Ms. Paterson alive."

"She was very much alive when I left her, and," Coleen said and held up her hand, "before you ask, I hadn't mortally wounded her, either."

"So you say, but none of the staff members report seeing her after your meeting. The Burkes claim she often came into the main building to check on guests in the evening, but she didn't last night, making us wonder if she wasn't alive to do so."

"But I didn't touch her," Coleen argued.

"Then you have nothing to worry about. If you're telling the truth, our investigation will reveal that."

Ha! Shannon thought. *Investigations often lead down rabbit holes.*

"What about a time of death?" Shannon asked, hoping to gain information to construct a better alibi for Coleen. "Has your medical examiner given you a preliminary time?"

"We believe it was early this morning, but I'm not at liberty to discuss the details at this point in the investigation." He turned back to Coleen. "Let's move on to your early morning departure. Leaving before anyone else was awake makes you look all the more suspicious."

Coleen crossed her arms. "I had to leave that early to pick up my friends at the airport."

Shannon looked at Coleen. "You must have your ferry ticket. Won't that have the time stamped on it? Or perhaps someone can confirm you were on the earliest boat."

Coleen shook her head. "I missed the first ferry and had to sit in my car to wait for the second one. I ... oh ... oh ... that's not good." Her face suddenly paled.

Watson leaned closer. "Which means you could have left at a much later time than you're claiming?" Shannon expected him to expound on his comment, but he suddenly stood. "That's all for now, Mrs. Douglas, but I'll have additional questions for you once we finish processing the crime scene."

Shannon looked up at him. "You didn't mention where Siobhan was killed or where you found her body."

"I didn't, did I?" He offered Shannon a tight-lipped smile. "Make sure you remain available, Mrs. Douglas. No more trips out of town without letting me know."

"I don't plan to go anywhere except into the village."

"Then we'll have no troubles." He saluted and headed for the door.

Shannon watched him go and couldn't get over how short the interrogation had been. Grayson would have been more thorough, and he would have provided a bit more information about the crime. Surprisingly, she missed Grayson and wished he were conducting the investigation.

"How do you think that went?" Coleen asked.

Shannon shrugged. "He's a hard man to read. Kind of like a chameleon."

"I thought the same thing." Coleen took a deep breath and blew it out. "Well, we're done with him for now, so let's put it out of our minds and move on to the wedding."

"I'm impressed with how well you're dealing with everything."

"There's nothing I can do about it. I'm not going to let it spoil the festivities." She got up and stretched her arms overhead. "Would you like to come with me to find Gemma, or do you need a rest?"

"Are you kidding?" Shannon forced energy she wasn't feeling into her tone. "I'm dying to see her."

"I was hoping you'd say that. I could use your help." Coleen tugged Shannon to her feet and winked. "Between you and me, Gemma's acting like a real bridezilla. The latest snag might push her over the edge."

"I'm glad to help defuse the situation if I can." As they exited the library, Shannon paused to admire the scrolling wood trim above the door. "This place is simply amazing."

"Isn't it?" Coleen replied. "I've been thinking I'm holding the wedding here as much for me as for Gemma."

"But of course you are. I totally understand that."

"Speaking of weddings." Coleen arched an eyebrow. "How's Michael these days?"

"He's doing well," Shannon replied, intentionally keeping her answer vague.

"Way to dodge the question."

Shannon grinned and hugged her friend close. "I did evade it nicely, didn't I?"

Laughing, they strolled into the grand hall. The sun had slipped behind thick clouds, darkening the room that had appeared so bright only a few minutes earlier. An involuntary shiver claimed Shannon.

"Och, we need to get you into warm woolens," Coleen said. "Right after we make sure Gemma hasn't had a meltdown. Then we'll sit down for a spot of tea and a long chat."

"Let's check to see if the Purls are still up and invite them to join us too."

"Deal."

"In all of this, you didn't mention if Ewan was here yet," Shannon said, finding it hard to believe she hadn't thought to ask about Coleen's husband until now.

"Och, no," Coleen said. "His mum isn't well, so he stayed back with her. He's still hoping she will be able to make the wedding, but he won't know until the last moment."

A tall, slender woman bustled into the foyer, followed closely by a striking man with silvery hair, black turtleneck, and neatly pressed trousers. The woman's piercing green eyes landed on Coleen. "Mrs. Douglas, I'm so glad we found you."

"Now what did I tell you about this 'Mrs. Douglas' business?" Coleen asked as she joined the couple.

"Yes, yes, of course, I forgot." The woman waved a manicured hand in the air.

Coleen took Shannon's arm and drew her forward. "Shannon, I'd like you to meet Fiona and Greer Burke, the amazing caretakers I mentioned to you."

Shannon gawked at the couple who looked more like models from a French fashion magazine than a pair of hardworking castle caretakers. Greer was dressed austerely and made a vivid contrast to Fiona, who wore an azure-blue pantsuit with a geometric-print blouse. She'd added a chunky silver necklace, earrings, and an arm full of bracelets. She reminded Shannon of Joyce, who was notorious for her bling.

Fiona laughed. "We get that look all the time. I suspect people think we don't belong at Hamilton Castle."

Greer smiled, revealing even white teeth. "The work here suits us, though. It gives us plenty of time and the means to pursue our true love."

"They're both artists." Coleen's words carried a healthy dose of awe. "Fiona paints, and Greer makes incredible sculptures. You'll see them around the castle."

Fiona waved slender fingers again. "Enough about us. We're a boring old married couple with hobbies to keep us busy."

Greer stepped closer to Coleen. "We'd hoped to have a word with you about the ... ah ... recent situation, if you have the time."

"Go ahead."

Fiona eyed Shannon. "Wouldn't you like to do this in private?"

Coleen laughed. "I have no secrets from Shannon. If I did, she'd simply worm the conversation out of me anyway."

"You're sure?" Greer asked.

"Positive."

Fiona's eyes narrowed, exaggerating the crow's feet near her penciled-in brows. "We just saw Inspector Watson out. He wanted me to tell you he intends to return tomorrow to speak with you again."

"Did he say about what?"

"No, but those forensics people apparently told him something interesting. He seemed excited. I suspect they found something in Siobhan's office that he wants to ask you about."

"Was she killed in her office?" Shannon asked.

Fiona shuddered. "That's where I found her this morning."

Coleen clasped Fiona's arm. "Oh, you poor dear, I didn't know you discovered the body. How are you doing?"

"I'm dealing with it."

Greer laid a hand on his wife's shoulder. "Don't let her kid you. She's still reeling from it, and I don't think she'll ever get over it. Nor will I forget her scream."

Fiona put a hand to her mouth. "This is shocking. Just shocking. Siobhan was the sweetest young woman. Never harmed a soul."

"What about the embezzlement?" Coleen asked. "I heard you talking about it last night."

"We have no proof of that. Only one woman's accusation."

"But you seemed so sure last night."

"And now that I've had time to think about it, I wish I hadn't said a word. That way you wouldn't have overheard us and wouldn't be in hot water with the police."

"Did they say Coleen was in hot water?" Shannon asked.

"Not in so many words," Fiona admitted. "I'm sorry, Coleen, but I heard you're a suspect, and I feel responsible."

"Nonsense," Coleen said firmly. "I didn't do anything wrong. I'll be fine."

"But what if the police come after you?"

"Shannon will make sure the real killer is brought to justice. I'll have you know, Shannon is quite the amateur sleuth." Coleen wrapped an arm around Shannon's shoulders. "In fact, she's solved several mysteries in the last year, and she'll be investigating Siobhan's death for me."

"Do you think that's such a good idea?" Fiona asked. "I find it best not to get in the way of the police."

Greer nodded his agreement. "We wouldn't want them to get angry and make them take longer in the investigation. Think of Gemma. They could hold up her wedding."

"Not to worry," Shannon said with confidence she

wasn't feeling. "I'll be discreet and respectful."

Greer harrumphed. "Then I'd best tell you that Inspector Watson expressly forbade anyone from entering Siobhan's office. Even us."

"Now that could be a problem." Coleen turned to Shannon. "We can't proceed with the wedding plans without Siobhan's files."

"We're OK there," Greer said. "Watson had one of his men make copies of her files."

Fiona smiled tightly. "I believe he's a romantic at heart, and he couldn't bear to see your sweet daughter's wedding go amiss."

Shannon highly doubted the dour inspector was a man overcome by sentiment, but at least the wedding preparations could proceed. In any event, she wouldn't let the caretakers sidetrack the murder conversation with wedding discussions. "Maybe you could tell us more about Siobhan. Did she have any enemies?"

"Our Siobhan?" Fiona clutched her chest. "No. No. Everyone loved her. Just everyone."

Obviously not everyone, Shannon thought but didn't say as she knew it would make them withdraw from her. "What about a boyfriend or ex-husband?"

"She didn't have a boyfriend, and she never mentioned being married." Fiona turned to her husband. "She would have told us if she'd been married before, wouldn't she?"

"Yes. She was a straight shooter." A fond smile much like a father would have for his daughter tugged at his lips. "She often talked about the lavish wedding she'd throw if she ever got married. I doubt she'd be that extravagant for a second marriage."

"Does she have family in the area?"

"Not here, but in Glasgow—that's where she grew up, the only child of doting parents. Oh no!" Fiona twisted her necklace. "Someone will have to tell her sweet mum and dad she's gone. They'll be devastated. Perhaps we should go visit them once Gemma's wedding is over."

"Good idea," Greer said, but his heart wasn't in his words.

Shannon hated to suggest to the distraught couple that the young lady they were painting almost as a saint might do something wrong, but she had to think of Coleen first. "Do you think Siobhan was capable of stealing?"

Fiona clamped her lips together. Greer glanced at his wife, then said, "We prefer to stay out of this if you don't mind. Siobhan was a friend, and we don't want to say anything we don't know to be fact."

Shannon could appreciate that, but she also had a murder to solve. "Could you tell me a little about her, then? Things you do know. Like where she attended school. How long she worked here, that kind of thing."

Fiona shook her head. "I'm afraid I'm not up to it."

"If you'll excuse us." Greer circled his arm around his wife. "I think it's time she takes a break. With Siobhan gone, she'll be taking on many of the wedding details in addition to her regular job." Greer smiled ironically. "I'd help, but what do I know about weddings other than my own?"

Fiona smiled up at him, then faced Coleen. "I know you must be worried about the wedding, but would it be OK with you if we waited until morning to get started on reviewing the details?"

"Absolutely," Coleen said. "You get some rest, and we'll talk after breakfast."

Greer led Fiona toward a hallway on the opposite side of the room. They glided across the floor, both with perfect posture. Shannon could easily imagine them dressed in formal attire and attending art galas and museums in the city.

"Do they live in the castle?" Shannon asked.

Coleen nodded. "They have a small suite in the back of the building."

"They seem nice."

"Didn't I tell you they are?"

"With her flamboyance, you better hope she doesn't want to make changes to the bridal plans. You might end up with one crazy-looking ceremony."

Coleen shook her head. "That's all my Gemma would need. Let's go tell her we're moving forward with the wedding plans."

Coleen set off at a rapid clip toward wide stairs lined with plush red carpet. "We're planning on taking some of Gemma's photos here on the landing. The glass will make a vibrant background for her gown."

Shannon joined Coleen on the landing and peered at the stained glass in bright blues, reds, and yellows. "Speaking of her gown, when do you want us to get started on the beading?"

Coleen started up the next set of stairs. "Tomorrow, if you're up to it after a long travel day." She looked back at

Shannon. "Please know that I don't plan for you and the Purls to work your fingers to the bone while you're here. I've also arranged sightseeing trips and other fun adventures. Assuming the girls are game, that is."

"I was hoping you'd say that. We have to give our friends a true introduction to the amazing sights this part of Scotland has to offer."

"And we can't let the murder investigation spoil their fun, either."

"I couldn't agree more."

Shannon climbed the stairs next to Coleen and entered a dark, narrow hallway with more flocked wallpaper. She felt the history of the grand old castle crowding down the hall, and she couldn't help but wonder about the stories the thick stone walls could tell.

Coleen paused and turned to Shannon. "Your room and the Purls' rooms are on this floor. I'm on the first floor in a small apartment with a kitchenette. Ewan's mum will stay with us, and she has so many food issues that we wanted to be able to prepare something for her to eat."

"And where is Gemma?"

"She has the bridal suite. Olivia is staying with her until the wedding."

"Oh, good. I get to catch up with *both* your daughters then." Shannon smiled with true delight.

"If you can take your eyes off the room long enough to talk to them."

"That grand, huh?"

"Wait until you see the suite. It's at the end of the hall and up another set of stairs in the tower." Coleen led the way to a set of circular stairs with a rough rope serving as the handrail.

As the coarse rope slid through Shannon's fingers, her imagination caught fire. "I can see the defenders of the castle climbing these stairs to watch for warring clansmen."

"They'd roll over in their graves if they knew their castle has been invaded by a bunch of women planning a wedding." Coleen cackled. Her laughter bounced off the walls and echoed up the tall column.

At the top of the landing, she knocked on a scarred wooden door. "Gemma, it's Mum."

The door whipped open, and Gemma launched herself into her mother's arms. The two were direct opposites. Gemma's more exotic look favored Ewan, as opposed to Coleen's girl-next-door wholesomeness.

"Oh, Mum. Finally. I've been going crazy here without you." Gemma wore a thick white robe, and she'd piled her shoulder-length, raven-black hair on top of her head. Soft ringlets, damp from a bath or shower, framed her face. Her pale complexion appeared almost white next to Coleen's more ruddy skin tone.

Coleen set Gemma away. "Let's talk about this in your room. OK, honey?"

Gemma looked up and finally noticed Shannon. "Oh hi, Shannon," she said absently and flounced into her room.

Shannon had expected a warmer greeting. After all, she'd known the girls all their lives, but she completely understood that Gemma couldn't focus on anything but her wedding right now.

Gemma plopped onto a four-poster bed made of heavy mahogany and boasting lacy white bedding.

Shannon took in the warm green walls, patterned draperies hanging on three tall windows, and the heavy antique furnishings. A tall stone fireplace glowed with a roaring fire, the shadows dancing over thick tapestry rugs. "Wow!"

"Auntie Shannon!" Olivia exclaimed as she rose from a satin settee in the corner. A lookalike for Coleen in her younger years, Olivia wore silk pajamas, the top a vibrant green and the pants flowery. Her hair, the same rustic brown as Coleen's, fell in soft waves over her shoulders.

"Sorry we're not dressed to greet you," she said, crossing the room. "Gemma wanted to soak in the tub and spend the night in the room. So I got comfortable too. I'm so glad to see you." She flung her arms around Shannon's neck. "You can save me from bridezilla," she whispered and then pulled back.

Shannon winked at the more easygoing of the sisters and squeezed her hands. "I'm afraid that's a task too big for any of us."

"What is?" Gemma asked.

"Nothing, sis." Olivia took a seat next to Gemma. "So, Shannon, tell us all about your new boyfriend, Michael."

Shannon groaned. "He's *not* my boyfriend."

"Right," Olivia said.

"Please." Gemma rolled her eyes at Olivia. "Someone *her* age wouldn't call the man in her life a boyfriend. That's too junior high."

Shannon sighed. "He's not a boyfriend *or* a man in my life. He's simply a friend."

"Uh-huh." Coleen entered the discussion. "We know better, don't we, girls?"

Olivia nodded. "Mum says he's devilishly handsome."

Shannon could hardly deny he was good-looking, but all the same, she felt the heat of a blush rise up her neck.

Olivia clapped her hands together. "Oh how cute. You're embarrassed. Then it's official, isn't it, Mum? She's smitten."

"Aye, that she is. Once she admits it to herself, we won't need to have these discussions."

"So," Shannon said, changing the subject, "tell me about your groom."

"His name is Sean Hurst, and he's amazing." A dreamy look replaced Gemma's irritation. "He's tall, handsome, and such a gentleman. Even Mum likes him, don't you Mum?"

"Aye, that I do." Coleen smiled. "You'll like Sean too, once you meet him. He's arriving later in the week."

Gemma suddenly frowned. "If there's a wedding."

"Of course there'll be a wedding," Coleen said. "Try to relax and not worry about this so much."

Hoping to take Gemma's mind off her problems, Shannon said, "This room is something right out of a fairy tale."

"You should see the bathroom." Gemma jumped up and led Shannon across the room.

They paused in the doorway, and Shannon took in the splendor. An oversized, copper-clad bathtub sat in the middle of the room on polished wooden floors, an antique vanity with two sinks next to it.

"I've soaked in that tub today until I'm a prune." Gemma looked up, her eyes watering. "This is just awful.

My wedding may be ruined, and to top it off, I can't get the thought of poor Siobhan out of my mind."

Shannon smiled at the younger woman. "Don't worry, sweetheart. Your mum and I won't let anything ruin your special day. And as for Siobhan, we'll find out who killed her. I promise."

Gemma flung herself into Shannon's arms. Shannon looked over her shoulder at Coleen. Her face was devoid of her usual cheerful smile. Shannon suspected Coleen's thoughts paralleled her own.

Gemma's wedding could very well be in the hands of the local police, and solving the murder in time might be the only way to keep Gemma's plans on target and Coleen out of jail, not to mention bring a killer to justice.

— 5 —

Yawning, Shannon crossed the wooden floor to answer the knock on her bedroom door. She walked past her magnificent bed and wished she could climb back in. She'd only gotten an hour or so of rest, and jet lag was setting in, but she was determined not to miss dinner with her good friends.

"I was wondering if you'd wake up in time for dinner," Coleen said as she bustled past Shannon. She wore dressy black slacks and a red sweater that made her appear less tired and stressed.

Shannon closed the door. "Trust me when I say I'd rather get more sleep than eat."

"This isn't just any food. We're having roast lamb with lovely potatoes and carrots. Everything is grown or raised right here on the property, so it's fresh and delicious." Coleen's stomach growled as if on cue.

"Don't worry." Shannon waved a hand. "I wouldn't miss our first dinner in the impressive dining room."

"Ready to get going?"

"Sure. Let me grab a shawl to keep the drafts at bay." Shannon dug out an emerald green shawl she'd knitted for the trip and draped it over her arm.

Coleen started for the door.

"Not that way." Shannon stepped to a tall mahogany bookcase. "We'll take the other route."

Coleen planted hands on her hips and looked at Shannon as if she'd lost her mind. "What other route?"

"This one." With a flourish, Shannon pressed a concealed latch on the bottom of a shelf, and the bookcase swung open, revealing a heavy wooden door.

Coleen excitedly clapped her hands. "How did you find this?"

Shannon pointed at a framed letter on the nightstand. "I went to make sure the Purls were up after I woke from my nap, and I found this letter when I came back. The owners encourage visitors to explore all the secret passages, so they put a letter in each room where one exists."

"Now I'm wishing I was up here with you instead of on the ground floor."

Shannon frowned. "Please don't say that. I feel guilty enough for having my own room when everyone else has to share one."

"With five of you, someone has to be alone. You all drew names for roommates, so it's totally fair."

"I know, but I still feel guilty." Shannon dragged the heavy door open. "Maybe I'll ask if anyone wants to trade rooms tomorrow night."

"That will make more work for the housekeeping, and they'll charge extra to change bedding."

"You're not saying that to make me stop feeling guilty, are you?"

"*Moi?*" Coleen clutched her chest. "I would never mislead you like that."

"Of course you would." Shannon laughed as she grabbed a battery-operated lantern from the wardrobe.

"There's no electricity in the passage." She stepped to the entrance and shone the light ahead, revealing a dark and winding staircase.

Heavy stones lined the walls, and well-worn stone stairs descended in a spiral. The space was colder, so Shannon spread her shawl over her shoulders and started down the stairs.

"What do you suppose the stairwell was used for?" Coleen asked.

"According to the letter, these stairs allowed the servants to travel throughout the castle without being seen by family or guests." In the dank, cold stairwell, Shannon could easily imagine the women in long skirts and uncomfortable shoes hurrying down the stairs to continue their life of service.

"This is such fun," Coleen said as they reached the first floor. "Having the wedding here is everything I thought it would be and more. I hope we have time to explore every inch of the place."

"We'll make the time even if we don't sleep." Shannon handed the lantern to Coleen and started running her hands over the rough wooden doorframe. "There's supposed to be a hidden block that opens the door."

Coleen lifted the light closer, and Shannon looked for any cracks in the wood.

A loud slam suddenly reverberated from the top of the stairs and filtered down.

Coleen spun. "Was that the door to your room?"

"Sounded like it." Shannon kept her focus on her task, but when she heard scraping on the floor above, she paused.

"I think someone's moving furniture in my room."

"But why? What if they're blocking the exit and we're stuck in here?" Coleen eased closer to Shannon and grabbed her arm. "Suddenly this isn't so wonderful."

"Relax. I need to find the right ..." Shannon pulled on a section of the wood, and the door shifted as if wanting to open, but it didn't move. Shannon pressed harder. Still no movement. "Help me push. I think something's blocking the door."

They both put their shoulders to the door and shoved. The wood groaned a bit, but refused to budge.

"Drat," Shannon said. "We'll have to use the door upstairs."

Coleen handed over the lantern. "Why would they leave the letter in your room if the door is blocked?"

"Good question." Shannon headed up the stairs and found that door closed too.

"Someone locked us in."

"The door could've swung shut in a draft."

"Something this heavy?" Coleen knocked on the heavy wood. "No way."

"I'm choosing to think it was an accident until we get out of here. Then I'll investigate the cause." Shannon ran her hands over the frame, but the wood felt like a solid piece.

"Are you sure there's a way back inside?"

"Of course. It will take a few seconds to find it. Maybe they hid the panel in a different spot."

"Let me do it." Coleen brushed past Shannon and quickly found the movable section. The door moaned but failed to open. "It's blocked too. Whoever put the letter in your room had to know you'd want to take the stairs."

Shannon shook her head. "We can't assume the letter was targeted at me."

"Of course we can. You'd checked in already, so anyone who worked on the staff would know this is your room."

"What difference would that make?" Shannon asked. "There's no reason any of the staff would want to harm me."

"Word that you're investigating could've spread through the group."

"Already? That seems quick."

"Trust me. I've been here for a few days, and I've heard gossip fly through the staff faster than a wildfire."

"I suppose you could be right. Especially if a fellow worker killed Siobhan." Shannon paused to consider what a killer working at the castle could mean.

"Exactly." Coleen planted her hands on her hips. "And they sealed us in. We're stuck."

"We aren't stuck. We can call someone."

"Get a signal in here? Are you kidding?" Coleen dug out her phone and held it up. "Nothing."

Shannon tried hers. "I don't have a signal either."

"What are we going to do?" Coleen's voice lifted high with anxiety.

"First of all, calm down and let me think."

Coleen shivered. "We're going to die in here. They'll find us. Two frozen popsicles."

Shannon imagined the sight and started laughing.

"How can you laugh at a time like this?"

"The stairs lead to the dining room, and the Purls will

gather for dinner soon. Let's head down, and we can pound on the door until someone hears us."

Coleen hissed out a breath. "Oh, right. Good idea."

Shannon led the way again, and at the bottom of the stairs, she heard voices. "See, I *told* you someone would be in there." She bent down to set the lantern on the stone floor, freeing her hands to pound. But when she moved closer to the partially open door, she heard people talking in frantic voices.

She peeked through a narrow gap. Greer stood next to Fiona, both of them holding a glass of wine. "The Burkes are in the dining room."

"Great. Let's pound on the door to get their attention."

"Wait." Shannon flashed up a hand. "They're talking about Siobhan. Let me listen for a minute in case they say something that will help us find the killer."

"I can't believe the police found the murder weapon so quickly," Greer said.

"I'm not surprised," Fiona replied. "It's unique, so it wouldn't be hard to figure it out. Even Constable MacGregor recognized it, and you know his skills in problem solving are very limited."

Greer laughed. "Definitely a small-town officer."

"Which is one of the reasons it's so lovely to live out here. Oh, wait—that didn't come out right. I mean that the people are genuine and laid-back, not that a small-town officer made it easy to commit a crime."

"What are they saying?" Coleen whispered.

"The police found the murder weapon."

"Did they say what it was?"

"No." Shannon put her ear to the crack again.

The lantern flickered on and off for a few moments, then extinguished. Coleen shrieked, making Shannon jump and nearly lose her footing. Shannon found the light and shook it to see if she could revive it, but the darkness remained. She could feel the walls close in on them, and the silence was even more deafening in the dark.

"That's it," Coleen announced. "I've got to get out of here, now." She pounded her fists on the door, the sound reverberating off the stone walls. "Help! It's Coleen Douglas. Help us! We're stuck in the hidden staircase!"

Shannon tugged on Coleen's sleeve until she stopped pounding. "Let's listen to see if they heard us."

"Mrs. Douglas, is that you?" Greer's voice was closer now.

"Yes! Yes! Please hurry. The door's blocked here and at the top."

"Hold on. I'll need to get help to move furniture out of the way."

Shannon leaned back against the wall. "I told you we'd be fine."

"That you did, but with the way trouble seems to find you, I wasn't so sure." Coleen collapsed onto a step and looked up. "Do you think someone was trying to stop your investigation already?"

"I don't know." Shannon had been thinking the same thing, but she didn't want to add to Coleen's worry. "The cold air is starting to get to me. Sharing body heat will keep us warmer."

Shannon felt around until she located the wide stone

stair and sat next to Coleen. Shannon could feel her friend shaking, so she distracted her by talking about wedding details until she heard furniture scraping over the floor in the next room. After what seemed like hours later, the door dragged back and light flooded through the opening. Coleen sighed out a long breath. Shannon rose, her muscles chilled and stiff. She helped Coleen to her feet, and they both slipped into the dining room just as the Purls were gathering there. Fatigue showed on their faces, yet their voices carried excitement.

"Thank goodness you're both all right!" Fiona exclaimed as she turned to the butler, who, like Greer, was now dressed in a traditional tartan kilt. "How on earth did this happen, Sheppard?"

The butler opened his mouth to speak, but Betty cried out from the other side of the room, "Look, ladies! A secret passage to explore."

Joyce headed straight for the opening in the wall. "Is that how you got downstairs?"

"Yes," Shannon replied without going into details.

"Now, don't think you can use the passage." Fiona stepped in front of Joyce, her elegant evening gown swishing on the floor. "It's been closed for repair for weeks now, and guests aren't allowed inside."

"But there was a letter in my room encouraging me to use it," Shannon said.

Greer ran a hand through his hair. "When the maid cleaned the room this morning, she must've forgotten it wasn't to be used and put out the letter. Isn't that right, Sheppard?"

"It's the only logical explanation," Sheppard answered in a dull monotone.

Shannon knew that conclusion was erroneous. "First off, the letter wasn't in there when I checked into the room, so the morning maid couldn't have left it. And secondly, with the tunnel closed for so long, why would she have the letter with her?"

Greer's brow furrowed. "I don't suppose she would, would she?"

Coleen lifted her chin and announced, "I think Siobhan's killer trapped Shannon in the stairwell to frighten her into backing off the investigation."

Kate took a few steps closer. "Do you really think so?"

"It wouldn't be the first time someone has tried to stop Shannon," Coleen said. "If I'm right, then the killer could still be in the house."

Melanie shuddered. "Please say you're kidding about this."

Fiona smiled, but Shannon could see it was forced. "Let's not jump to conclusions. It could simply be a mistake."

"Hah." Coleen's expression turned skeptical. "How does someone *mistakenly* move heavy furniture in front of an open passage door?"

"Simple," Greer said. "The evening maid came to turn down the bed and saw the door ajar. She realized it shouldn't be open, so she got someone to help her secure it."

"We'll question the staff right away," Fiona offered.

Not buying Greer's explanation, Shannon faced him. "Who would know about the stairway and have access to the framed letter?"

"Everyone who's ever worked here and anyone who has ever visited would know the stairwell exists," he answered. "I suppose the number of people who knew it was closed off would be limited to our current staff."

"And the framed letter?" Shannon asked.

"It's kept in the supply room, and everyone on staff has access to it."

"Then I'd like a list of the staff members who are on duty tonight."

"I don't know." Fiona glanced at Greer. "Wouldn't that be a privacy violation?"

"Indeed it would. Allow us to look into this for you." Greer turned to Sheppard. "Would you be so good as to talk to the workers to see who might've been in Mrs. McClain's room?"

Sheppard nodded. "Right after we move this bookcase back into place so no one discovers the stairwell on this end and gets stuck in it again."

As they started sliding the heavy case, halting tones from a bagpipe cascaded down the hallway.

"What in the world is that for?" Kate asked.

"You Americans might consider this the dinner gong," Fiona said humorously. "You'll also receive a similar wake-up call in the morning with a serenade through the castle."

The sound grew louder, irritating Shannon's ears. Though she'd grown up in Scotland, she'd never adjusted to the harsh notes emanating from bagpipes.

Fiona gestured at the table. "If you ladies will be seated, I'll see that your dinner is served. We're starting with a lovely roasted pumpkin soup followed by a fillet of Angus beef with a port wine."

"Sounds wonderful." Joyce rubbed her tummy. "I'm ready for another traditional Scottish meal."

The piper strolled into the room dressed in full Gaelic attire—a kilt, tartan over his shoulder, and kneesocks. He slowly paraded around the room, then marched back out the door like he'd not seen them.

"I love it here." Joyce linked arms with Shannon and stepped toward the long table set with formal linens and antique china.

What Shannon wanted to do was check her room for clues left by theperson who'd barricaded them in the stairwell. But she didn't want to be rude and leave her guests behind, so she allowed Joyce to lead her.

Joyce pulled out the head chair. "As our unofficial tour guide on our first-ever Scotland trip, this spot is perfect for you."

"Don't bother pulling it out for her," Coleen said dryly. "She's going to run up to her room to look for clues before sitting down to dinner."

Shannon flashed her friend a surprised look.

"What?" Coleen laughed. "I know you're dying to do so, and you'll be distracted through dinner if you don't. So get it out of your system and then join us."

"Do you mind?" Shannon surveyed the group.

"Coleen's right," Melanie said. "Go ahead."

"Thank you." Before they changed their minds, Shannon darted out the door and hurried across the grand hall to the staircase.

As she climbed the stairs, she couldn't let go of the feeling someone was watching her. She stopped and spun but found no one. She let her imagination run wild, searching the large family portraits on the wall for a person peering through the eyes of a painting.

Finding nothing amiss, she shook her head. "Relax," she whispered to herself, but despite the encouragement, she *knew* someone was watching her. She just didn't know who—or if they intended her harm.

— 6 —

Shannon loved seeing the rare winter sunshine filtering through the drawing room window. It filtered over Coleen and the Purls, who had moved chairs into a circle in the middle of the room. They'd spread out Gemma's gown in front of them. The glorious morning rays bounced flashes of light from the needles as the ladies added beads to the full skirt. The Swarovski crystals on the hand-beaded lace bodice sent sparkles dancing around the room.

As Shannon approached, she heard Coleen humming *I Love a Lassie*, a traditional Scottish song that Shannon had heard often in her childhood.

"This dress is simply breathtaking," Shannon said, bringing an end to the song. "I would never be able to tell it from an expensive gown in a posh store."

Coleen looked up, pride beaming from her face. "It *is* amazing, isn't it?"

Shannon cast a longing look at her friends' handiwork. "I wish I could join all of you."

"And we wish you could help us too, but Coleen needs you more right now." Melanie quickly adjusted her glasses, then returned to work.

"The dress is in good hands." Coleen stood, and as she came around the circle, she paused to squeeze each woman's shoulder and compliment her work. She retrieved her tote bag from a small desk in the corner.

Betty glanced up for the briefest of moments. "I suppose you're off to question the Burkes about the embezzlement?"

Shannon nodded. "I saw Fiona heading toward the office, so we should be able to catch her there."

Melanie met Shannon's gaze. "After the incident last night, you should both take care."

"Aye, we will." Coleen slung her bag over her shoulder, her smile fading away.

Shannon circled her arm around Coleen and hugged her close. "Don't worry so much. We'll be fine."

"Hah," Coleen said as she slipped free and started for the door. "You keep telling me that, but being stuck in that stairwell, plus the past attempts on your life, makes me a bit jumpy. I won't rest easy until the murderer is caught."

Shannon caught up to Coleen. "Then I need you to do your very best to persuade Fiona to talk with me."

"That I can do." She slowed and stared pensively into the great room. "I'll start by talking about the wedding, then smoothly transition to the subject of Siobhan."

Shannon groaned. "Maybe you should leave the change in subject to me. Smooth transitions are not your strong suit."

"Me?" Coleen clasped a hand to her chest. "I'm the epitome of smooth."

"In your dreams, my friend. Only in your dreams."

Coleen broke out laughing, then sped through the grand hall, her mirth ringing through the cavernous space. Nearing the office, she patted the side of her tote bag. "By the way, I have the information on Gemma's accounts that you asked for. I hope it will help us solve the case."

"Me too, but don't expect too much. I should imagine if

Siobhan was embezzling, she covered her tracks quite well, and we may not find anything amiss."

"Maybe we could have Michael look at them."

Shannon watched her friend for a moment. "You actually want his help, right? You're not trying to play matchmaker again?"

"As a professional, he'd know what to look for." A mischievous smile took hold of Coleen's mouth. "Of course, if it helps love run its course, then I'm even more in favor of involving him."

Shannon gently thumped Coleen's forehead. "I knew there had to be an ulterior motive in there somewhere."

"But of course." She chuckled. "In all seriousness, what would it hurt to give him a call?"

Shannon pondered for a moment. "He would be helpful, but I hate to run to him all the time. Let me take a look at the file first, and if I think his input is needed, I'll call him."

Coleen swatted her hand at Shannon. "Spoilsport."

"A girl's gotta do what a girl's gotta do," Shannon called after Coleen, who'd started for the office.

Down the chilly, shadowed hallway, they found the Burkes' office door standing ajar. Fiona's pleasant voice drifted through the opening. Shannon peeked inside and spotted Fiona sitting on the edge of an organized desk, talking on the phone. She wedged the phone against her neck, beckoned them with a crooked finger, and then cleared a stack of folders from one chair and a pile of unopened mail from another.

As Fiona continued her conversation with a bride-to-be,

Shannon glanced around the room. Large contemporary paintings in vivid primary colors adorned three of the walls. Abstract sculpture took up most of the credenza.

Shannon nodded at the artwork and whispered to Coleen, "Fiona's work?"

Coleen nodded. "She's very talented, isn't she?"

"Yes, and that might make a great topic to use to butter her up."

Call concluded, Fiona issued a deep sigh and dropped into her high-backed chair, looking very much like a deflating balloon. "I hope you aren't here to report a problem too."

"Rough morning?" Coleen asked.

"Word's getting out about Siobhan, and brides are starting to panic." She pressed her thumb between her eyes. "I'll get through this, but only by the skin of my teeth."

"I'm sure the castle owners will be able to find a replacement soon enough."

Fiona dropped her hand. "I'm not so sure. We were lucky to get Siobhan. Most wedding planners don't want to live in the middle of nowhere."

"You seem to like it here, however," Shannon said. "Maybe you can use that to convince someone to join the staff."

"Maybe." Fiona cast a skeptical look at Shannon, then glanced at her watch. "Did I get the time wrong for our meeting to review the wedding details? I thought we were getting together right before lunch."

"We are," Coleen replied. "But I wanted to ask about the … the ah … the …."

"The minister." Shannon jumped in to save her friend from failing miserably in her attempt at a smooth transition.

"Is he a local clergyman, or is he coming from Glasgow?"

"Local. Why?"

"When will Gemma and Coleen be able to meet him?" Shannon continued.

Fiona looked baffled, but she grabbed a business card from the desktop and handed it to Coleen. "Here's his contact information. Gemma can call and set up an appointment with him, but I must say, it's unusual in destination weddings to meet the minister before the rehearsal."

Shannon searched for a logical explanation to her offbeat topic. "With Siobhan's passing, it's comforting to be able to confirm details wherever possible so the wedding goes off without a hitch."

Fiona nodded, a silver necklace laden with charms clinking as she moved. "I completely understand."

Coleen picked up the thread of the conversation. "Speaking of Siobhan's murder, could you give us the names of all the brides for the last few months and the ones coming up in the next few months?"

"Whatever for?" Fiona asked.

"They'd have motive for murder if Siobhan embezzled from their accounts. With their contact information in hand, Shannon could ask about their accounts and find out if they have alibis for the time Siobhan was killed."

"I see," Fiona said, her frosty expression saying she still didn't intend to talk about Siobhan.

Shannon slid forward. "I realize it would be highly irregular for you to disclose the information, but this is an unusual situation."

"Be that as it may, there are privacy issues, and you have

no official status. I'd rather leave the investigation to the police to sort out." Fiona stood. "Now, if you'll excuse me, I'd like to go to my studio and work off a bit of my stress before the next call comes in."

Feeling a bit like a naughty schoolgirl caught misbehaving, Shannon got up and followed Coleen out of the room.

"That could've gone better," Shannon whispered in the hallway.

"I was sure she'd help."

"I think she wants to, but she's a stickler for her privacy rules, which I suppose her job requires."

"Maybe Greer might tell us more," Coleen suggested as they stepped into the grand hall.

"Good idea. Any thoughts on where we might find him?"

"I saw him working in the garden Sunday. Maybe he's there again today."

"Gardening at this time of year?"

"It looked like he was tilling the dead plants into the soil." Coleen nodded at the stairs. "We can see if he's in the garden from the window in your room."

"I'd need a jacket anyway, so let's take a look."

In her room, Shannon crossed the open space, looking at every item to see if anything had been disturbed. When checking her room after the stairwell incident last night, it appeared as if someone had rifled through her things. The wardrobe's contents could've been disturbed when it was moved, but the items in her tote bag were also jumbled. Since she and Coleen had heard someone moving the wardrobe, she'd expected to find it in front of the stairwell, but finding the framed picture gone had been a total surprise.

Perhaps Greer had already had it removed, or maybe the killer had taken it while they'd been trapped in the stairwell to cast doubt on Shannon's story.

No matter who took it, she now made sure she left every item in a specific place so she could tell if anyone had been in the room. Spotting nothing amiss, she glanced out the window. The sun was now cloaked behind dark clouds threatening a downpour.

Coleen joined her. "There he is. On the right. By Siobhan's cottage."

In the distance, Shannon spotted a worn one-story cottage with a large garden to the side and a man dressed in tweeds turning the soil. "Please tell me you saw him from the window Sunday and not on your way to Siobhan's cottage."

"I wish I could." Guilt flashed in Coleen's eyes.

"You've been in her home?"

"Yes. She asked to see me around lunchtime on Sunday, but when I got to her office downstairs, she wasn't there. So I went in search of her. Fiona told me Siobhan had gone to her cottage. I was worried something had gone wrong with the wedding plans, so I trekked out there. Turns out I could've waited. She wanted to tell me the groomsmen's gifts were arriving that day, and she wondered if I wanted to look at them."

Shannon sighed and pondered the implications of Coleen's actions.

Coleen clasped Shannon's arm. "Is that bad news?"

"Maybe. I doubt guests often visited Siobhan in her home. If the police lift forensic evidence proving you've been there, it could add to their list of reasons to suspect you."

"But I only stepped inside the door for a moment."

"Can you prove that?"

"No. Of course not."

"Do you think Greer saw you at her cottage?"

Coleen looked out the window. "If he did, I need to know if he told Watson about it." She turned back. "Grab your coat, and we'll ask him."

Fearing rain, Shannon pulled her fleece-lined jacket from the cupboard, and Coleen grabbed a similar water-proof jacket from her room. Outside, they walked along a narrow path on the edge of a bluff overlooking the sea loch.

"I love the view," Shannon said, "but I don't like how close we are to the edge."

"What happened to the confident woman who told me everything would be fine?"

"She still believes it will be fine, but she doesn't like the thought of slipping and plunging into the loch."

"I won't let you fall." Coleen tucked her arm in Shannon's and tugged her closer. "At least not without going over the edge with you."

Shannon chuckled but carefully watched each step. When a harsh wind kicked off the ocean, she moved closer to Coleen for warmth. They both put their heads down to cut the biting wind.

Despite the warmth of Coleen's body, Shannon shivered. "I forgot how cold the wind can be on the islands."

"Aye. The temperature may be moderate today, but the windchill is another story."

They hustled forward until they descended into a slight valley where the wind eased off. Away from the ocean now and in an open meadow, Shannon and Coleen picked up speed. When they reached the area recently tilled by Greer, they separated to climb safely over the clods of rich brown soil.

Greer glanced up but kept tilling. Despite the threat of rain, he wore only an old tweed jacket with leather patches on the elbows and a matching cap. Mud covered his wide-wale corduroy pants.

As they approached, he stomped his pitchfork into the ground with a worn boot. "What brings you ladies way out here in the awful weather?"

"We were hoping to have a word with you about Siobhan's case," Coleen said bluntly before Shannon could ease into the conversation.

His smile fell. "I thought I made it clear yesterday that we won't be talking out of turn about her."

"We don't actually have questions *about* her." Shannon jumped in and gave Coleen a let-me-handle-the-questioning look. "We're more interested in finding out if you saw anything unusual in the last few days."

He stripped off his work gloves. "Unusual in what way?"

"Did you see anyone in places they weren't supposed to be?" Shannon asked. "Strangers on the property? That sort of thing."

He raised his face in thought, then looked straight at Coleen. "I suppose your trip to Siobhan's cottage Sunday was out of the ordinary. Can't say as guests often visit the staff cottages." He paused for a minute and leaned on the end of the pitchfork. "In fact, I can't remember a time when a guest came all the way out here for any reason other than to see the vegetable garden."

"She asked to see me," Coleen said defensively.

"At her cottage? Seems unlikely."

Coleen crossed her arms. "She wasn't in her office."

"I don't suppose you noticed Coleen didn't stay but a moment?" Shannon asked before Coleen could start arguing with Greer and ruin their chance to question him.

"Aye, that I did. You'd barely stepped inside before the two of you came rushing across the field. Is that important?"

Shannon didn't want him to place any importance on the situation, so she shrugged. "Did you witness anything else out of the ordinary?"

"Not that I can think of."

"Will you think about it and get back to me if you come up with anything else?"

"I suppose." He pulled the pitchfork from the soil, then paused with it in midair. "But I warn you, if it's important enough for me to bring to your attention, I'll also be telling Inspector Watson. I won't hide *anything* from him."

"We wouldn't want you to hide information from him," Coleen said, though her voice wavered.

"Glad to hear that."

"We also hoped you could help us locate a list of the brides," Coleen barreled on.

"I'm afraid that's Fiona's department, and I'm sure she wouldn't breach confidence by giving you such a list."

"That's why we're coming to you."

He shook his head vigorously. "Why would I go behind my wife's back?"

"That's not what we're asking you to do," Shannon said. "But you could try to persuade her to provide the brides' information."

"Not my Fiona. Once she has her mind made up, it's impossible to change it." He jabbed the pitchfork in the soil for emphasis.

"Can you think of another way we can get the information?" Coleen asked.

He lifted his cap and scratched his head before settling the brown tweed back on his head. "I suppose you could go into the village and speak with the minister and priest who've presided over many of our ceremonies. They might be willing to give you the information you need."

Coleen clapped her hands, the sound echoing over the countryside. "Great idea, Mr. Burke. Thank you."

"I concur," Shannon said. "Please be sure to let us know if you think of anything else that can help."

They stepped away from him, and when they were out of his earshot, Shannon said, "As much as I wish he could have been more helpful, it's refreshing to see such an honorable man in today's world."

Coleen nodded firmly. "Agreed. The Burkes are a lovely couple, and under different circumstances, I could see us being friends."

They retraced their steps across the meadow, the wind slapping Shannon in the face as they crested the hill. She tucked her chin down, watched her feet, and didn't look up until they neared the castle and moved away from the bluff's edge.

Coleen pointed at the driveway in the distance and frowned. "The police are back."

"Hey," Shannon said. "Don't let this worry you. We knew Inspector Watson was coming back today."

Though a deep crease formed between Coleen's eyes, she pulled back her shoulders. "You're right. I won't let this ruin my day."

"That's my girl."

At the driveway, Shannon hurried Coleen past the white Land Rover with a blue light bar on top and vivid blue and yellow stripes on the side before her friend lost her confidence.

In the grand hall, they found Watson deep in conversation with Fiona. When Shannon closed the door, they both looked up.

"There she is." Fiona stabbed a finger in their direction.

"Good day, Mrs. Douglas," Watson called out. "I was hoping to have a word with you."

He crossed the space, and after an apologetic look for Coleen, Fiona scurried toward the hallway leading to her office. Watson wore the same rumpled trench coat. It hung open, revealing a navy button-down shirt, red tie, and a green cable-knit sweater.

"I'm glad you're here, Inspector." Shannon wanted to have the upper hand in the conversation, so she marched up to him with purpose in her stride. "I wanted to inform you of an incident that happened here last night."

"An incident?"

"Coleen and I were taking one of the secret passages to the dining room when someone blocked the exits, trapping us inside."

"Mrs. Burke has already given me all the details. I doubt it has anything to do with Ms. Paterson's demise. Sounds like an honest mistake to me."

Shannon fought back a flash of anger at his dismissing tone. "We're not of the same opinion. We're thinking if the killer is a staff member, they may have used this as an opportunity to warn me to back off my investigation."

"Ah, yes, that," he said with a smirk in his voice. "I'd heard you're looking into things."

"And clearly you don't think me capable of helping at all," she blurted out before she could tame her frustration.

"Murder investigations are best left to the professionals." He sounded exactly like Grayson, only with a thick Scottish brogue, and his doubt in her abilities made her pull up her shoulders. But she knew it wouldn't do any good to argue with him.

"Did you have questions for me, or can we go?" Coleen asked, her tone on the surly side.

"We believe we have found the murder weapon."

"Believe?" Shannon asked pointedly.

"We're waiting on confirmation from the casualty surgeon on the match, but we do know Siobhan was stabbed with a cylindrical item about one inch in diameter." Watson paused, his gaze zeroing in on Coleen. "Can you think of anything in Siobhan's office that might fit this description?"

"I don't know why you're asking me. I'm not that familiar with Siobhan's office." Coleen frowned.

"I have it on good authority that you're familiar with this particular item, as it involves your daughter's wedding." He waited, watching her carefully.

Tension filled the space as Coleen chewed on her lip and pondered his comment. A spark of recognition suddenly lit her eyes before she quickly masked it. Shannon doubted

Watson witnessed the flash, but Shannon knew her friend well enough to know Coleen was hiding something.

"It's hard to think with you staring at me," Coleen finally said to Watson. "Perhaps you could give me time to think about it."

"Of course," Watson said, eyeing Coleen with suspicion. "I have a few additional staff members to interview. We can meet again after lunch."

Coleen nodded woodenly.

Watson didn't miss the change in Coleen's demeanor this time, but he said nothing as he departed.

Shannon eased closer to Coleen. "What is it?"

"Knowing that Siobhan was killed in her office, I'm pretty sure the murder weapon is a wine-bottle stopper from a lovely rosewood accessories box Sean is giving to his groomsmen."

"A wine stopper? Seems odd. Would it be sharp enough to kill someone?"

"This one is. It's part of a set to go with the castle theme. All the tools are of a medieval design and have pointed, sharp ends."

"Let's say you're right. Why not tell Watson that?"

"These are the same gifts Siobhan showed me the night before she died. Each box has an engraved nameplate on top. I wanted to check out the quality of the gifts. The box for Sean's best man, Craig Stewart, was on top of the stack, so I took out the stopper and inspected it. I put it back in Craig's box when I was done, but I'm positive I left the box open. Assuming the killer grabbed that stopper to kill Siobhan, my fingerprints will be all over the murder weapon."

Shannon's heart sank.

Coleen wrapped her arms around her waist. "Watson already suspects me, and the fingerprints are sure to put me at the top of his list. If he even has a list beyond me."

Shannon wanted to offer words of comfort, but Coleen was right. Fingerprints on the murder weapon would not only firmly place Coleen on the suspect list, but they could also cause her to be arrested for the crime.

— 7 —

Near lunchtime, Shannon and Coleen sat with Fiona in her office. They were working through wedding details, but the need to find a solid lead kept Shannon's mind fixed on the crime. With Coleen's prints on the murder weapon and a sketchy alibi, Shannon believed it would be only a matter of time before Watson arrested Coleen. But what could she do about it without concrete clues to follow?

She'd already phoned the town's two clergymen, but both were out of their offices, visiting sick parishioners, so they couldn't meet until tomorrow. If only there was another way to obtain the brides' names.

"Shannon," Fiona said, "are you with us?"

"Sorry. I drifted off for a minute. Where were we?"

"We were divvying up Siobhan's wedding-day duties, and we've reached the guest book. Do you think one of your friends would take charge of it?"

"I'm sure they'd all be happy to—wait, that's it!" She swiveled toward Coleen. "Can you excuse me for a minute? I'll be right back."

Coleen eyed her. "With that look on your face, even if I insisted you stayed here, I know your mind would be elsewhere."

"Thank you." Shannon started to rise, but when she caught Fiona's disapproving scowl, she stopped.

Coleen gestured toward the door. "Go ahead. Get out of here before I change my mind."

Shannon didn't need any more encouragement, and she took off for the grand hall. She'd passed the large credenza near the front entrance several times, but the book sitting on top hadn't registered until Fiona mentioned Gemma's guest book.

She picked up the thick, gilded book and opened it. Each page held a place to write the guests' names, addresses, the dates of their stay, and any comments they wanted to offer about their visit.

Footsteps clipped down the hallway and Shannon looked up. When she saw Coleen, Shannon said, "I thought you had more details to discuss."

"Fiona got another call from a distraught bride, so she asked to take a break until after lunch. What are you up to?"

"Fiona's comment about the guest book made me remember the registry for castle guests." Shannon held the book out and ran her finger down a page. "See how the last names are listed over and over again on certain dates?"

Coleen nodded. "And that means what to you?"

"We can assume there was a wedding that day and these guests are from either the bride's or groom's side of the family."

"They have other gatherings here."

"But the pattern of two prominent last names suggests we're dealing with a wedding."

"And if we call some of them, they might give us the bride's name, and we can track her down." Excitement built in Coleen's tone.

"Exactly." Shannon slapped a high five with Coleen. "It will be a long shot, but it might be worth the effort."

"Absolutely."

Shannon glanced at her watch. "Let's go meet the Purls for lunch and see if we can enlist their help."

"My thoughts exactly." A spring in her step, Coleen took off at a clip that spoke to her newfound hope.

Shannon put the guest book back on the credenza and joined Coleen, who was greeting the Purls outside the drawing room.

"Hurry up, Shannon," Melanie called out. "Gemma is modeling her dress so we can evaluate our work."

Shannon hurried to catch up to the group.

Melanie moved into place next to Coleen. "We're hoping you'd give us your opinion of how it turned out."

"I'm eager to heap my praise on you," Coleen said enthusiastically.

"But you haven't even seen it yet."

"I'm happy to see my Gemma in her gown, but I don't need to see the dress to know you'll have done me proud." She let her gaze travel over the group. "I'm so blessed to know each and every one of you and to call you friend."

The others returned the sentiment, and despite all the turmoil surrounding Siobhan, Shannon felt her heart swell with happiness. Misty-eyed, she followed the ladies into the dining room. A long buffet table sat to the side of the room, laden with dishes emitting pungent aromas into the air, warm breads, and salad fixings. Gemma stood on a low platform as Olivia arranged the long train of her dress. Gemma's face radiated happiness, her eyes alight and shining nearly as brightly as the crystals on her dress. She moved gently, like a soft wave undulating against a shore, and the overhead lighting caught the crystals, casting brilliant sparkles of light through a room otherwise shrouded by the downpour outside.

"Oh, Gemma, what a captivating sight you are!" Coleen clapped her hands to her mouth and tears glistened in her eyes. She rushed to her daughter and ran her fingers over the crystals on the bodice. "It's lovely. So lovely. The workmanship is exquisite."

"You're a bit prejudiced though," Joyce said with humor in her tone.

"I know quality when I see it." Coleen spun to face the Purls. "I can't believe you've finished the work so quickly."

"Goes to show you what happens with the power of the Purls behind you," Shannon offered, sniffling back her own tears of joy.

Coleen smiled at the women circling around her. "I don't know what I'd do without you here to keep my sanity."

"Please, Mum, don't be so dramatic," Gemma said.

"Spoken by the world's greatest drama queen." Olivia made a face at her sister. "Is there anything I can do to help with the wedding plans, Mum?"

"Thank you, but no," Coleen said. "Taking care of Gemma is the best thing you can do right now."

A young waitress dressed in a period costume bustled into the room carrying a large urn, which she set on the buffet table. A blend of savory spices, including rosemary, scented the air behind her. She looked up at Gemma and a longing expression captured her face. "Might I say, miss, you are a vision. I've never seen a dress more perfect for a castle wedding."

"See?" Coleen announced. "An unbiased opinion of your work, ladies."

The Purls preened, and Shannon was even more proud of the dress than if she'd made it herself.

"Please help yourselves to the food." The waitress curtseyed. "I'll be back to take your drink orders momentarily."

Closest to the buffet, Melanie lifted the urn's lid and looked inside. "C'mon, ladies. It's a lovely stew. Perfect for the cold weather."

Olivia's stomach grumbled loudly. "I'll help Gemma change, and we'll be back to eat in a flash."

"What are you thinking?" Gemma asked sharply. "I can't consume all those calories and still fit in my dress. Nor can you. We'll have salads in our room."

Coleen took Gemma's hand. "Perhaps Olivia could have a wee bit of the stew."

"Mother," Gemma chastised. "I'm the bride, and I know what's best for the day."

"It's OK," Olivia said. "I'd love to have another salad."

Shannon listened for any sarcasm in Olivia's tone, but she appeared sincere as she lifted Gemma's train and helped her from the room. Olivia clearly took her maid-of-honor duties seriously, and despite Gemma's self-centered attitude, Olivia wouldn't let her sister down.

"Your Olivia's a real peach," Shannon said to Coleen as she joined the others at the buffet table.

"Don't I know it. Gemma's usually one too, but this week I don't even recognize her."

Betty set her sewing bag next to a chair and joined them. "I went through the same thing with my eldest. Gemma will be back to normal after the wedding."

Coleen took Betty by the shoulders and looked into her eyes. "Promise me this is sure to happen."

Betty chuckled. "Trust me. I've known lots of brides who went through this stage, but they usually come out the other side a well-adjusted woman."

"Enough of the small talk, ladies," Kate said as she passed by, holding a plate laden with food. "Fill those plates. I'm famished." She took a seat at the table, which was long enough to seat sixteen people, and looked at Coleen. "Any update on Siobhan?"

Coleen filled them in on the morning's developments. She left out the information about handling the murder weapon, however. Shannon supposed she'd omitted it to keep from ruining the jovial mood in the room, and Shannon wasn't about to bring it up for that same reason.

Melanie picked up a plate of fresh apple pie. "What happens in the investigation now?"

"Shannon called the clergymen who perform the ceremonies," Coleen said, "but both of them are out of the office until tomorrow. We plan to head into the village to talk with them then." Coleen grabbed a delicate soup bowl. "And you, my wonderful friends, will be joining us for a bit of sightseeing."

"Are you sure there's time for that?" asked Joyce. "We've got so many wedding details to take care of."

Coleen heaped her bowl with steaming stew. "Thank you for thinking of the wedding first, but I will not ruin your trip by keeping you locked up in here."

"As if sitting in a wonderful castle could be considered a hardship." Betty put her plate on the table and gestured around the space. "I mean, look at this room. I could study the intricacies of the tapestry drapes and the expertly woven rug for days and not tire of any of it."

"And there's always the secret passageways to explore," Joyce added.

Coleen shook her head. "You won't get me in one of those again."

"Was it that bad?" Betty sat next to Kate at the near end of the polished table.

Coleen shuddered. "Worse. I'd rather not sit in pitch-black darkness, wondering if I'll ever get out or if some madman is coming to do me in."

Shannon felt like making a face as Olivia had done a moment ago. Clearly, the apple didn't fall far from the tree.

"Don't mind her." Shannon ladled stew into her soup bowl, which was ringed with tiny decorative roses. "She's putting her usual dramatic spin on the situation."

"Maybe a tad." Coleen headed for the table, her expression turning sheepish.

"I do want to go on record as saying that drama aside, there's no one I'd rather be stuck behind a wall with." Shannon winked at her friend as she grabbed a crusty roll to go with her stew and then joined them at the table.

Melanie forked a bite of potato and blew on it. "Well, I for one can't wait to explore the place."

Betty took a bite of the stew, which was loaded with vegetables and venison. "This is heavenly."

"Well, eat up, ladies," Coleen said. "I need you all in top form, as I have to impose on your kindhearted spirits again this afternoon."

"More wedding details needing work?" Betty asked.

Coleen launched into their plan to review the guest book and make phone calls. "I need to catch Gemma up on details from my morning meeting after lunch, and Shannon hopes to interview the castle staff. So if a few of you could give up beading the skirt for research, it would be most helpful."

"Why don't we work in shifts?" Betty offered. "Joyce and I can start making the calls you mentioned and then, after an hour, switch with Melanie and Kate."

"Perfect," Shannon said. "I'll show you where the guest book is right after we finish lunch. Since we can't get a reliable cell signal in the building, we'll need to copy down the information and then go outside to make the calls. With any luck," Shannon said, crossing her fingers, "we'll be on our way to finding a viable suspect."

8

Feeling like a quarterback releasing her team from the huddle, Shannon dismissed the Purls, and they scattered from the grand hall. Betty and Joyce were on their way to find a notebook to record data from the castle guest book. Melanie and Kate headed back to the drawing room to work on the dress. Coleen had started for the stairs to talk with Gemma, but she'd planted her foot on the bottom step, stopped, and was staring into the distance.

Shannon followed her gaze to Inspector Watson, who was striding down the hallway toward Coleen. He carried a large paper bag and trained his laser-sharp focus on Coleen, who looked like she might wilt under the heat.

Shannon hurried over to her friend and warned her quietly. "No matter what he says, keep your cool."

"How can I?" A chord of unease threaded through her voice. "He'll want to know if I have any idea about the murder weapon, and I'll have to tell him about the gifts."

"All you can do is tell the truth." Shannon stepped closer to Coleen. "I'm right here with you."

"Ladies." Watson greeted them with a smile. "I've conducted my interviews and even had a chance to follow up with Greer." He faced Coleen. "He mentioned that you'd gone to visit Ms. Paterson at her cottage. It seems odd that you trekked all the way out there."

Coleen crossed her arms and explained what had

happened. "I was only there for a few moments, as I hope Greer also told you."

"He did mention that, but he didn't say why you would visit Ms. Paterson."

"She wanted to show me the groomsmen's gifts, which had just arrived."

"Interesting," he said and tapped his chin. "Do you know why I find it interesting?"

Coleen opened her mouth, then clamped it closed and swallowed hard. Obviously, she didn't intend to say that she believed Siobhan was killed with the wine stopper, and Shannon feared Watson would find her at fault for impeding the investigation.

"Perhaps it would help if you gave us a better idea of what you're thinking, Inspector," Shannon said.

With a measured glare, he set the bag on a gleaming mahogany table and slipped on a pair of latex gloves. Gloves meant the bag held evidence—evidence that could implicate Coleen in the murder. With a flourish, he opened it and drew out a gleaming rosewood box. His focus never left Coleen as he made a great show of setting the box in front of her. He ran his fingers over the nameplate, which was labeled "Craig Stewart," much like a model might do with a grand prize on a game show.

Coleen planted her hand over her mouth and stared at the box like it belonged to Pandora herself.

He slowly opened the box, his gaze still riveted on Coleen.

A strangled cry slipped from her mouth, and she suddenly dropped onto a step.

Watson leaned closer. "I see you know the importance of this particular box."

Shannon squatted next to Coleen and held her hand. She sat up straighter and took in deep breaths. While Coleen finished composing herself, Shannon glanced in the box. The bottom held a single wine bottle boasting an expensive-looking label. Rigid foam filled the lid, and cutout sections held an assortment of wine-serving tools. The slot Shannon assumed would hold the very pointed bottle stopper was empty.

Watson pointed at the hole. "The coroner compared a bottle stopper from another gift box to Ms. Paterson's wound. He confirmed that the wound she died from is consistent with having been made by a stopper like the one that is missing."

"I imagine it's helpful to know how she was killed," Shannon said, trying to buy time until Coleen could collect herself.

Watson nodded. "Especially when we were able to lift several viable prints from this box." Watson bent closer to Coleen and waited for her to look up and meet his gaze. "One of my men will take your prints before we leave today, Mrs. Douglas. Do you suppose we'll have a match?"

Shannon silently willed Coleen to admit the truth. If she didn't and Watson discovered it later, Shannon could easily predict the kind of trouble Coleen would be in with the inspector. Trouble that could result in an arrest.

"It's possible." She drew her knees up and wrapped her arms around them. "I looked at this very gift box Sunday when they arrived."

"Looked at?"

"Handled them. We purchased them on the Internet, and I wanted to make sure they were of good quality."

"As you now know, they are quite solid." Watson came to his full height. "At least solid enough to end someone's life."

He'd been reserved in his questioning until now, but his tone had turned antagonistic, and Coleen didn't need the additional tension.

"I think it's time to move on," Shannon said. "Coleen has told you everything she knows about the set and the missing stopper."

Watson looked at Shannon like she was a buzzing mosquito he wanted to swat, but he nodded and returned his focus to Coleen. "Perhaps we can talk about your alibi. We've set the time of death on Monday between 5 and 6 a.m. You claimed to have departed from the castle before five, but we've been unable to find anyone at the ferry to corroborate your story."

Coleen's chin rose and her usual fire returned to her eyes. "I told you yesterday that I missed the first boat and had to take a later one. It was a chilly morning, so I sat in my car. Someone must have seen me in the parking lot."

"I hope you'll continue to look for someone who saw her there," Shannon said.

"We'll keep after it … at least until we find the murder weapon. But be warned, Mrs. Douglas. If we find your fingerprints, and if we still can't verify your alibi, then I'll have no choice but to arrest you for murder." He paused as if waiting for Coleen to respond, but she said nothing.

"Please keep in mind Coleen's daughter is getting

married on Saturday," Shannon said, hoping to end the conversation amiably. "We'd appreciate it if you'd respect this very important time in their lives."

He nodded. "My daughter married last summer, and you have my solemn promise that I won't make an arrest until I'm confident of obtaining a conviction."

Though his comment could mean he would gather enough evidence to bring Coleen to trial, Shannon chose to ignore the double meaning and thanked him for his consideration.

He packed up the box and started for the front door, but suddenly stopped and turned. "If my daughter's recent wedding is any indication, I know you'd never leave your daughter and flee the area, Mrs. Douglas. Nevertheless, I feel like I must warn you not to go anywhere without first consulting with me."

Coleen nodded and forced a smile. "Thank you." Her tone was lighthearted, but she'd balled her fingers into a tight fist.

"One must do what one must do to keep the bride happy and not falling to pieces." He chuckled and stepped outside.

Shannon waited to speak until the door closed. "That went as well as could be expected."

Coleen released and flexed her fingers. "I agree, but I had to bite my tongue so many times to keep from saying the wrong thing that I think it's raw."

"Don't take this the wrong way, my friend." Shannon stood and tugged Coleen to her feet. "I'm glad your tongue is raw. Otherwise you might be in hot water with Watson."

"And hot water could lead to a jail cell," Coleen said solemnly. "Not a place I want to be." She dusted off her pants. "I need to check in with Gemma, but come find me if you learn anything from Fiona."

They split up and Shannon located Fiona in her office. The door was ajar, so she poked her head inside. "Do you have a minute?"

Fiona crossed her arms and sat back. "Greer told me you talked to him this morning. I won't change my mind about giving you the list of brides, so don't bother trying to worm them out of me."

"I understand," Shannon said sincerely. "But I'm here for a different reason."

Fiona gestured at the chair without mounds of paperwork piled on it. "Sit."

"I was hoping you'd agree to introduce me to the staff on duty so that I might ask a few questions about Siobhan."

"Greer manages the staff, and I'm sure he wouldn't want you to disrupt their work."

"I promise not to be a distraction."

"I don't know."

"Please," Shannon said. "Every hour that passes brings Watson closer to believing Coleen killed Siobhan, and I've made no progress in helping her." Fiona's expression softened a tad, giving Shannon hope. She pounced on the opening. "You must have a good friend that you'd do anything you could to help out of a mess."

"Yes, but—"

"If you were in my place and someone could help you, what would you do?"

Fiona thought for a moment, then said, "Fine. The kitchen staff will be eating lunch right now, and I suppose it wouldn't hurt if you talked to them while they're on break."

"Thank you." Shannon shot to her feet before Fiona changed her mind.

Fiona led the way through the interior of the castle, the air growing more dank and pungent as they moved down the maze of hallways. Thick stone walls ringed the kitchen, but modern commercial appliances and fluorescent lighting brightened the space. A wooden table sat at the end of the room where five staff members ate the same venison stew Shannon and her friends had eaten for lunch. As she approached, the workers swiveled to look at her, their faces a mix of curiosity and interest.

"This is one of our guests, Shannon McClain," Fiona announced. "She would like to ask a few questions about Siobhan."

Expressions quickly turned skeptical.

"I'm sorry to interrupt your break," Shannon jumped in, "and I promise not to take up much of your time."

"I'll leave you to it," Fiona said. "Would one of you please escort Mrs. McClain upstairs when she's finished?"

"I will," a portly woman with flaming red hair said. "I'm Rhona, the head cook. Please join us." Her chubby face lit with a smile as she held out her hand to an empty chair.

Shannon perched on the cane-backed chair at the end of the table and shivered under a cold draft coming through the door at her back.

"Och, that chair won't do. You'll catch your death of

cold." Rhona turned to a young man seated nearby. "Be a gentleman and give up your seat for the lady, Jimmy. You're a tough one, and you can handle sitting by the cellar door."

Shannon shook her head. "That's not necessary."

"No bother." Jimmy stood, his freckled face crinkling with a smile.

Shannon moved to his chair.

"Can we offer you some tea?" Rhona asked.

"I don't want to trouble you."

"No trouble at all." Rhona let her gaze travel up to Jimmy's face. "Fetch a cup while you're up."

Jimmy shook his head. "Switch chairs. Fetch a cup. You're worse than me mum."

"I don't need any—"

"You'll have your tea." Jimmy winked at Shannon. "I don't mind getting the cup. It's the nagging I mind."

"Youth today." Rhona swatted a hand at him. "They've got a mind of their own." She turned her startlingly blue eyes on Shannon. "Now what is it we can help you with?"

"I was hoping one of you might have an idea of anyone who would've wanted to harm Siobhan."

"Holly Taylor," Rhona said and received murmurs of support from the others. "Siobhan got her fired a few weeks ago, and she spewed her hatred at Siobhan."

Shannon pulled her notebook from her tote bag. "Do you know why she was fired?"

"Not officially, but she was late to work frequently. Maybe Siobhan got tired of being shorthanded at the receptions when everything needed to go like clockwork."

"Do you know where I might find Holly?"

"She's renting a home in the village, but I don't know the address." Rhona looked around the group. "Anyone else know?"

Shaking heads provided the answer.

"Is there anyone else who might want to hurt Siobhan?" Shannon asked.

Rhona shook her head. "Everyone at work liked her, except Holly. I don't think she had much of a social life. She dated occasionally but didn't have a serious boyfriend."

"Sounds like a lonely life," Shannon said.

"No, no," Rhona said. "She wasn't a hermit, if that's how I made her sound. She'd head into Glasgow whenever she had several days off in a row. Maybe someone she knew in Glasgow had it in for her."

Since Fiona had also mentioned Glasgow, Shannon jotted down the city next to Siobhan's name and looked around the group, hoping someone would volunteer more information. No one spoke up, so she said, "Thank you for sharing. If you think of anything else, you know where to find me." Shannon stood and dropped her notepad and pen into her bag.

"Is it true someone closed you in the passageway to the dining room last night?" Jimmy asked.

"Yes."

Rhona shared a knowing look with Jimmy.

"Is there something you're not telling me?" Shannon asked.

Rhona shrugged. "Not really."

"Then what was with the look?" Shannon asked, not willing to let her evasive behavior go.

"If you were locked in the stairway—and if it was the killer who did it—then I doubt the person you're looking for is in Glasgow," Rhona answered, and Jimmy nodded his agreement. "I'd wager an entire month's salary the killer is either working here now or has worked here in the past."

Shannon found her logic to be sound. Now all she had to do was prove it.

— 9 —

Shannon flung back the downy quilt on her bed and sat up. She'd tossed and turned enough for one night. Her internal clock was all out of whack from jet lag, and she'd spent the last three hours trying to count sheep. Instead, she found her mind wandering over the mystery surrounding Siobhan and worrying that Watson might soon arrest Coleen. If only Michael were here. She could run the details by him and get his opinion on how to move forward.

Should she call him? It wouldn't be a bad thing to hear his voice—of that she was sure. And when he'd said good-bye, he *did* say he was going to miss her.

She glanced at the clock and quickly calculated the time difference with Oregon. She imagined Michael seated alone in his den, reading a book or working on one of his many reports for his security business.

Before she could talk herself out of it, she quickly dressed and grabbed her jacket. She hated to go outside late at night, but the hilltop near the castle boasted the only reliable cell signal. Phone in hand, she stepped into the hallway. The fireplace in her room had made it toasty warm, and in comparison, the hallway felt cold and dank, like the secret passageway. Uncertainty halted her steps for a moment.

"Get a grip," she whispered. "It's not like the killer is sitting out here, waiting for me to get up in the middle of the night."

Still, she hurried along the hall and down the main staircase. Muted lamps lit the grand hall, leaving it shadowed and unwelcoming and increasing her unease. She searched the nooks and crannies beyond the heavy furniture and found herself alone.

What had she expected?

She shook her head as she opened the front door. She'd never felt this uneasy before. Maybe Coleen's vivid imagination and concerns were catching. Or maybe the swords and guns mounted on the walls along with the coat of arms were fueling her mind's wanderings.

She used the flashlight on her cell to make her way to the hill. As soon as she had enough bars on her phone, she hit the speed dial for Michael.

"Shannon!" he said with enthusiasm on the fifth ring. "Glad to hear from you. I assume you arrived safely in Scotland."

"Without a hitch."

"You must be exhausted by now. It's, what …" He paused. "Two in the morning there?"

"It is, but I can't sleep, so I thought I'd ask if you could help with a problem."

He groaned. "Please don't tell me you've run into another mystery begging to be solved. I'm not sure I can survive seeing you through another one."

She chuckled at his tone, one that lacked conviction. "If I don't tell you about it, how am I going to get your help?"

A long sigh filtered through the phone line, and she wondered if he was actually upset about the latest mystery.

"I understand if you'd rather not talk about this," she said, lightening her tone. "I can tell you all about Gemma's dress, her lovely flower arrangements, the cake, the—"

"Stop," he said with a laugh. "No man should have to listen to those details except for his own wedding, and even then it's iffy."

She grinned and launched into the facts of Siobhan's death. When she'd finished the tale, including what they'd discovered so far, she waited to hear Michael's thoughts. She didn't have to wait long.

He sighed. "I wish I could give you better news, but if they're able to lift clear prints and they match Coleen's, it doesn't sound good for her."

"My thoughts exactly. Do you think her arrest is imminent?"

"Imminent?" he asked. The phone fell silent for a moment. "I can't speak to the way an investigation is handled in Scotland or to any evidence your inspector hasn't shared. Do you know if there's another person of interest in the case?"

The light on her phone extinguished and blackness overtook her. "I'm not aware of another suspect, but Watson tells me even less than Grayson."

"And it's driving you crazy."

"A bit."

Michael snorted.

She stifled a flash of irritation. "OK, fine. It *is* driving me crazy, and I would appreciate your help so I can overcome it."

"Well, if I were investigating, Coleen would be on the top of my suspect list. But before arresting her, I'd start with the basics and look for motive. As you know, there's always a motive for murder. I'd ask myself if there is sufficient evidence to indicate probable cause to a reasonable and prudent man of Coleen's guilt."

"I'm pretty sure it's reasonable to assume that if Siobhan stole Coleen's money and the wedding of Gemma's dreams had to be cancelled, Coleen might lose control and harm Siobhan. Though I think it's a bit of a stretch."

"Ah, but stress could make an otherwise reasonable mother snap, especially the week of her daughter's wedding."

Shannon hated to admit it, but he was right. "True."

"Once motive was established, I'd look at the physical evidence. Without the murder weapon, I'd ask if DNA was located under Siobhan's fingernails from struggling with the killer. Or did she bite or otherwise wound her attacker? I'd carefully review all trace evidence collected at the crime scene."

Shannon sighed. "I'd love to be able to tell you about that, but as I mentioned, the inspector hasn't provided any details."

"OK, but it's hard for me to make a judgment without knowing everything."

"Could you speculate?"

"For you, of course," he said, and she could hear genuine affection in his voice. "If Coleen's prints are the only physical evidence, I'd wonder if I didn't arrest her now, could she corrupt other valuable evidence."

A bitter wind raced over the hill, and Shannon turned her back to it. "I suppose she could, but it's not likely. The office where Siobhan was killed is locked, but Coleen has access to the rest of the estate."

He didn't respond right away, and she could imagine his usual pensive look as he worked through the ins and outs of the case before offering advice. "So what you're saying is that she could know about evidence elsewhere and try to retrieve it."

Shannon sighed. "Yes."

"I'm sorry, but you wanted my honest opinion."

"I did. At least I thought I did when I dialed the phone." Misty rain started falling, and she flipped up her hood.

"I could make some inquiries with the police if you'd like," he offered. "Since I'm a former detective, they're more apt to cooperate with me than with a civilian like you."

Was it a good idea for him to ask questions? She thought about Watson and doubted he'd take kindly to interference. "If you were the detective on this case, how would it make you feel if someone did that?"

"Honestly?" he asked. "I'd be miffed."

"Exactly. And if Watson found out we had a professional looking into the case, he could take it out on Coleen."

"If he's a good cop, he won't, but that's always a possibility."

"Please don't call then. At least, not yet."

"If that's what you want."

"It is, but I could use your help with the bills and statements for Gemma's wedding. If I can get them scanned, I could email them to you for review. I don't see anything that suggests embezzlement, but your trained eye might find something."

"I'll be glad to look at the information."

"I'll try to get them to you first thing in the morning."

"Great. And feel free to call me if anything changes. I'll do what I can from here."

Though she'd have liked to talk to him longer, the rain started picking up, and she had to get inside before it soaked her. But after the call ended, Shannon instantly missed the comfort of his voice. Her sudden emotion caught her by surprise. She'd come to rely on Michael over the months and even had feelings for him, but did they go deeper than she thought? Coleen said they did.

Shannon shook her head. These questions were best avoided in the wee hours of the morning when she needed to get some sleep. She flipped on her flashlight and raced down the hill. Inside, she shook the rain from her jacket and realized the outside air had invigorated her, making her sleeplessness even worse. What she needed was a good book to occupy her mind, and the library shelves held a great assortment.

She hung her jacket over a chair to dry and headed for the library. A small night-light near the door gave only enough light to see without knocking her shins on the heavy furniture. She made her way to the floor-to-ceiling bookshelves, which were lined with classics. A sign stated guests were free to read the books, but they couldn't take them from the library. It had been a while since she'd read a Jane Austen novel, so she selected *Pride and Prejudice* and settled into a thickly padded chair. Betty would be proud.

A musty odor filled the air as soon as she cracked open the worn, leather-bound book. She imagined a woman in the eighteen hundreds reading by candlelight, and she quickly immersed herself in the book.

Suddenly, a loud thumping noise sounded from below, startling her. Another thump, like someone had slammed a heavy door in the cellar, broke the silence again. Was the killer on the move, maybe planning harm to someone else?

Shannon came to her feet and eased toward the door.

The sound of someone dragging a heavy object filtered through the floor. Not normal noises for four in the morning, she supposed. But maybe normal for Hamilton Castle.

Maybe it wasn't the killer, but the staff starting work. But would they be at work so early? They didn't serve breakfast for hours. Surely it didn't take hours to prepare the meal.

Could someone be in trouble? If so, Shannon had to see if she could help.

She glanced around the room, looking for a weapon, and spotted a wrought iron fireplace poker. Grabbing it, she slipped into the hallway and waited for her eyes to adjust to the dim light.

The scraping sounds grew louder as she neared the door leading to the kitchen. Darkness and silence cloaked the room, heavy like the damp air. No staff members sitting in front of a warm fire like yesterday. No warm smells of breakfast scones baking. No whistle of a teakettle.

Shannon ran her fingers over the rough stone walls to find her way. Slowly, she crept toward the cellar door, one foot in front of the other, sliding across the cold stone floor. Voices whispered up the stairwell, swirling toward Shannon and then disappearing before she could recognize them. She leaned her head toward the doorway and cupped her hand around her ear. Mere whispers. Nothing to identify them. Maybe a man and a woman, but she wasn't sure. She moved closer.

Another thump resounded though the floor. Shannon jumped and dropped the poker. It hit the floor with a solid clang that reverberated through the room. Great. She'd given herself away and left herself unprotected. She dropped to the frigid stone and groped around for her makeshift weapon.

She reached ahead, and as her fingers landed on the wrought iron, she heard footsteps climbing the stairs. Heavy, solid footsteps. *Thump, thump, thump.* They pounded closer. A man, for sure. The killer?

Her heartbeat kicked up, thudding in her chest as solidly as the footfalls stomping closer. A sliver of light spilled under the thick door. He was almost upon her. She scurried behind the massive island in the center of the room. Ducking down, she gripped the poker and held her breath.

The door swung open, the light rushing into the darkness. She wanted to stand and identify the person, but she couldn't risk discovery. He stepped into the room. Her pulse sped up, racing beyond control.

Her breath came in shallow bursts. She tossed up a quick prayer for safety and waited.

"Is someone there?" the male voice asked.

Greer. Was it Greer?

She wouldn't show herself until she was certain of his identity. She scooted to the side of the island and peeked around the end.

"Mrs. McClain?" Greer said, his eyes going wide.

Relief washed over her at the sight of a friendly face. Her breath rushed out, and she gulped another.

He came closer, the lantern shining bright. "What on earth are you doing down here?"

"I couldn't sleep," she said, coming to her feet. "I went to the library to read and heard a noise. I was worried someone might be in trouble."

"So you grabbed a poker and came down here." He shook his head, then chuckled. "You really *are* quite the sleuth, aren't you?"

She nodded and smiled, though with her knees feeling like they might give way, she didn't feel like a capable detective. "Would have been a better sleuth if I hadn't dropped the poker and given myself away. I hope I didn't damage the floor."

"I doubt it; the stone's pretty tough."

Shannon tried to inspect it, but the light was too dim. They should turn on the lights. *Why were they out anyway?* "Why are you down here, and why the lantern?"

"We had a plumbing issue, and we had to cut off some of the circuit breakers because of the water. We had to move a few storage bins before the plumber could get to work, but we should be right before breakfast."

His explanation explained the noises she'd heard, and she felt a flush of embarrassment creep up her neck. "I guess I overreacted."

He chuckled again. "Happens to many of our guests. They let the folklore of ancient times spark their imaginations."

"I'd like to say that's all it is, but Siobhan's death brings an added dimension to this situation."

He frowned. "I imagine it does. Perhaps you'd rest easier if you left the investigating to the police."

Shannon shook her head. "I won't rest until I've located the killer and made sure Coleen's name is cleared of any wrongdoing."

"She's lucky to have such a good friend." He gestured at the doorway with the lantern. "I'll escort you back upstairs."

He didn't have to say another word to convince her to let him lead her out. She'd had quite enough of darkness, dank corners, and frightening encounters tonight. She only hoped the unsettling event was the last one she experienced during her castle stay.

— 10 —

Dappled sun filtered through the early morning clouds, settling on the winding country road to the village. Fond memories of Shannon's many visits to the area with her father warmed her heart on the chilly day. Her father could spend days exploring the glacial valley, and Shannon had loved traipsing along with him and learning about the area.

"There's the village!" Joyce exclaimed as the town came into view. "How delightful!"

"I agree." Betty's face glowed with happiness. "With the lush scenery and rain, I was beginning to think we were back in Oregon, but we don't have centuries-old buildings like these back home."

Shannon nodded. "Each shop has a story to tell. The oldest building in the village dates back to the sixteenth century, but it's nothing more than ruins now." Shannon turned to Coleen. "Why don't we park in front of Stitches so the ladies can put their purchases in the car instead of carrying them around town?"

"You're that sure they're going to buy something, are you?" Coleen slowed as she neared the yarn shop.

"Of course I am. No true knitter ever passes up the opportunity to get their hands on authentic Shetland wool yarn."

"That's akin to a deadly sin," Melanie added, sounding serious.

"Exactly," Kate said. "This is the closest we'll ever be to

where the sheep are raised and the yarn spun."

Coleen bumped the minivan to the curb. "Of course, you could all come back next autumn, and we could travel up north for Shetland Wool Week."

"Wouldn't that be a treat?" Betty said longingly. "But my budget doesn't allow two international trips in one year. Not to mention, Tom would kill me if I left him alone to manage the inn again."

"I doubt any of us can afford another trip, so let's make the most of our visit to this quaint little shop." Joyce slipped into her jacket.

"Shannon and I'll head to the church," Coleen said, "and we'll meet you at the Hamilton Country House for lunch. You'll find it at the end of the street and up the hill on the right."

"Hill?" Melanie cast a skeptical look ahead. "Looks like more than a hill to me."

"Hey, it's not like we're asking you to climb an actual mountain like Goat Fell," Shannon said. "That would be the highest mountain on the island. This is a bit of a hike, but the brisk winds and the climb will give you an appetite for the delicious food."

"I'm game for a bit of a hike. I'm still stiff after all that time on the plane." Betty dragged open the side door, and the Purls slipped out, their gazes going up and down the street of whitewashed shops, all boasting colorful signs.

Melanie held up her camera. "I need a group picture before we head our separate ways."

The ladies gathered under the scrolled Stitches sign, and Melanie snagged a passerby to snap the picture.

After a few shots, Melanie retrieved her camera. "I'll take a few more inside."

The Purls entered the yarn shop, and Shannon fell into step next to Coleen. They strolled down the main road, then turned onto a side street with an uphill path. By the time they reached St. Bride's, Shannon was out of breath and had to stop for a moment at the edge of the property, which boasted a small white church with a cast-iron bell in the belfry.

"Maybe we spoke too soon about climbing up to the Country House," Coleen said while gasping for full breaths.

"Maybe, but I won't be admitting it to the others. They think we're made of sterner stock than this." Shannon set off for the main entrance, the door groaning its age as she pulled it open.

They found the minister, an elderly man with a shock of white hair and chapped cheeks, at the pulpit, his head down as he spouted a fiery sermon into the cold air. He didn't look up or acknowledge their presence.

Shannon meandered down the short aisle and cleared her throat.

He looked up, then rushed down the steps. "Och, forgive me for not noticing you." He stuck out a hand as red as his cheeks. "Liam Anderson."

Shannon took his icy hand and introduced herself and Coleen. "I appreciate your willingness to meet with us on such short notice."

"I'm happy to help." His eyes narrowed. "I can hardly believe our dear Siobhan has gone to heaven."

"Can you think of anyone who'd want to kill her?" Shannon asked directly.

"Och, no. A sweeter soul you've never met. All the brides and families loved her." He turned his focus on Coleen. "I daresay you and your daughter found her to be most pleasant to deal with."

Coleen nodded, but she said nothing. Probably a good thing, as the minister didn't need to hear about Siobhan's alleged embezzlement.

"I hate to rush you along," he said, looking at his watch, "but I'm late for a hospital visit. If you'll follow me, I'll show you the records you requested."

He took off at a surprisingly brisk clip for his age. He exited the sanctuary and wound down a narrow hallway with whitewashed walls. The temperature dropped as they moved deeper into the building, eventually reaching his office, where a modern space heater cast out the chill.

"Please have a seat," he said as he unearthed a leather-bound book from a drawer and flipped through gold-trimmed pages. "Though I'm not the family minister, I have the bride and groom register so I can check in with them during their first year of marriage." He frowned and shook his head. "I take my role seriously. You'd be surprised how many marriages are on the verge of failing that soon." He laid the book open in front of Shannon.

She noted the first entry was six months ago with weekly entries in the summer, then falling off as the weather cooled. She looked around the room for a photocopier, but the modest room held no modern conveniences except the space heater.

Shannon looked up. "Do you have time for us to jot down the information?"

He glanced at his watch again. "If you're quick about it. Mrs. MacDonald should be coming out of surgery any minute, and I want to be there for her."

Shannon dug a notepad out of her bag and tore off a few pages for Coleen. "We'll do the brides only starting from the most recent date and working our way backward. You start on the left, I'll do the right."

"I'll return to working on my sermon and come back for you in ten minutes sharp," Liam said, hustling out the door.

Coleen flexed her fingers. "I wonder if public marriage records have phone numbers associated with them? If they did, we wouldn't have to copy all this information."

"We'd have to make an appointment at the county registration office to get the records. That could take days." Shannon eyed Coleen. "You know as well as I do that we don't have time to wait."

"Aye, so let's get to work."

After both of them had copied several pages of names, Coleen lifted her hand and stretched her fingers. "I'm assuming you're planning to call all these brides."

Shannon nodded.

"That might be a challenge, with the castle landline for emergency purposes only and cell service spotty up there." Coleen laid a hand on Shannon's to draw her attention. "We could fax or email our list to Michael, and he could make the calls."

"Overseas?"

"With clients all over the world, he's bound to have an unlimited calling plan."

"I don't know," Shannon said, pondering the idea. "I

don't want to take advantage of him."

"Don't think of it that way. Having him make the calls would free us up to investigate other avenues and still have some fun with the Purls. Plus it'd give you an excuse to call him again."

"How do you know I've called him?"

Her lips split in a sudden grin. "I didn't until you confirmed it."

Shannon swatted her hand at her friend. "I'll think about it. Now back to work."

"Do more than think about it. Do it. Your day will brighten when you hear his voice, and you'll be glad you did."

As much as Shannon wouldn't admit it aloud, thinking of talking to Michael again brought a smile to her face—and he had said he'd help in any way he could.

A knowing look crossed Coleen's face. "Ah, I can see you're thinking about him."

Shannon forced her mind onto the names in front of her, but she felt a flush of heat warm her face.

"Isn't that sweet," Coleen said. "Blushing at your age."

Shannon ignored the comment and busied herself with recording the names. By the time the minister scurried into the room, they'd worked through the last two months. Couple the information with the guest book, and they should have plenty of data for now.

He snatched up his book and secured it in his desk. "Remember your promise on the phone to keep the information confidential, and to use it only for this investigation."

"Absolutely," Shannon said, and she meant it. She'd had

to work hard to convince him to supply the brides' information, and she wasn't about to betray that confidence.

"I'll walk down to the village with you." He charged for the door.

"I guess this is how he stays so thin," Coleen said. "Maybe I need to start moving faster."

"But then you wouldn't have time to meddle in other people's affairs."

"I wouldn't, now would I?" Coleen's feet slowed. "And speaking of meddling, did you decide if you're going to call Michael?"

"Not that it's any of your business," Shannon said, "but I agree that it might be a good idea to ask him to help us."

"Excellent," Coleen said, the wind stealing her word and whisking it out to sea. She tucked her chin down, and they followed the minister's racing speed down the hill.

At the bottom, he turned and said, "I'm assuming you'll want to see Father Baker next."

"He wouldn't agree to give us the brides' contact information," Coleen blurted out.

Liam cringed. "Perhaps I was a bit hasty in being so free with it."

"Not at all." Shannon reassured the man. "You wanted to help bring the person who killed Siobhan to justice. That's an important way you can minister to her even after she's gone."

"It is, isn't it?" He sounded like he needed to convince himself of the fact and could easily ask them to return the information they'd copied and make them wait for an appointment at the county registration office.

"Do you happen to know where Holly Taylor lives?" Shannon asked quickly before he requested they hand over their notes.

"There're not many souls in town who don't know where Holly lives." He rattled off directions and, still concerned he'd change his mind, Shannon didn't ask him to explain why everyone knew Holly, but instead thanked him and pulled Coleen away before she said anything else unhelpful.

Bucking the cold, they traveled through the streets and arrived at Holly's dilapidated rental cottage in no time. Knee-high weeds peppered the yard, and despite the copious amounts of rainfall since the fall, the grass was a sickly brown. Paint chipped from the whitewashed cottage, revealing the rock foundation of the old building.

Coleen *tsked*. "I'd never allow Gemma or Olivia to live in such a ramshackle place, and I daresay you wouldn't let Lara either."

"I hope she never has to experience something like this, that's for sure." Shannon picked her way up the crumbling stone walk. "Let me do all the taking," she said to Coleen with a pointed look. She knocked on the door, releasing flakes of paint that swirled away in the wind.

The door was jerked open by a young woman with jet-black hair and heavily made-up eyes. "Yeah."

"Are you Holly Taylor?" Shannon asked.

She ran her gaze up and down Shannon, then crossed her arms. "If you're here about an unpaid bill, get in line. I lost my job, and I don't have the money."

"We wanted to talk to you about Siobhan Paterson."

"What's that control freak done now? Ruined your

daughter's wedding or something?"

"Actually, she was murdered."

"What? When?" Her arms fell to her sides and she gaped at Shannon. Her surprise felt real, but then, she wouldn't be the first killer to feign shock.

"Two days ago."

"Guess I've been holed up here for too long if I missed that news." She scratched her greasy scalp. "Where'd it happen?"

"In her office."

"Most likely had to do with work, then." A snide smile found its way to Holly's lips. "Guess she got what was coming to her."

With every word that came out of her mouth, Holly moved up on Shannon's suspect list. "Your name keeps coming up in my investigation as the only person who might want Siobhan to come to any harm."

Holly raised her chin. "Don't believe everything you hear. Siobhan had plenty of enemies. At least there were plenty of people willing to bad-mouth her behind her back."

"Care to give us a few names?" Coleen asked.

Holly eyed Coleen like she was first seeing her. "Exactly who are you ladies, and what business is this of yours anyway?"

"My daughter is getting married at Hamilton Castle this week. I was the last one to see Siobhan alive, so the police are trying to pin her death on me."

Shannon wouldn't have been so forthcoming, but it was too late to put the genie back in the bottle.

"I see," Holly said as she turned her attention to Shannon. "And you?"

"She's the person who's going to keep me out of jail."

Coleen's words rang with pride. "Now, about those people who were bad-mouthing Siobhan."

Holly's eyes clouded over for a moment as if she warred with the decision of what to reveal. "Start with her former boyfriend, Owen Reid. He's the reason I got canned. She couldn't handle the fact that he flirted with me when he was with her."

"But she didn't have a—"

"Where can we find Owen?" Shannon butted in before Coleen called Holly a liar and caused her to clam up.

"Works at the distillery." She turned her wrist, which was circled with a snake tattoo, and looked at a Goth-style watch. "He's about halfway through his shift by now." She started to close the door.

Shannon grabbed the doorknob and pushed back. "One more thing before we go. Where were you on Monday between 5 and 6 a.m.?"

"Where would you expect me to be at that time of day? I was here. Sleeping."

"Can anyone confirm that?"

"No, but then I didn't kill Siobhan, so why would anyone need to confirm that I was home?" A knowing look captured her face. "You suspect me? For real?"

"Just covering all our bases."

"Look, I mighta hated the lady for getting me fired for no good reason, but killing her for that would be lame." She jerked the doorknob from Shannon's hand. "We're done here." She slammed the door. Flakes of paint rained onto Shannon's boots.

"You believe her?" Coleen asked.

"Oddly, I do," Shannon said reluctantly.

"But the Burkes said Siobhan didn't have a boyfriend."

"Perhaps the Burkes were mistaken. Wouldn't be the first time an older person was kept out of the loop regarding a romance."

"True. Almost takes a miracle to get my girls to confide in me nowadays." Coleen frowned. "We have time to visit the distillery before we meet the Purls if you want to talk to this Owen fella. Holly said he'd finished half his shift, so maybe we can catch him on his lunch break."

"Good idea." Shannon met Coleen's gaze. "Don't you find it odd that Siobhan's recently been murdered and the boyfriend's back at work so soon?"

Coleen tapped her chin. "Now that you mention it, that is odd. Either he *isn't* her boyfriend, or he's callous enough to be the one who ended her life."

"My thoughts exactly." Shannon linked her arm with Coleen's. "Let's go find out which one applies."

— 11 —

Waiting for Owen's supervisor to retrieve him from the break room, Shannon walked through the distillery's visitor center. She'd never paid much attention to whisky distilling, but she found the history of illegal whisky smuggling on the island fascinating.

"Who knew the purest water supply in all of Scotland was found on the north coast of Arran?" Coleen asked as she read about the process of distilling the whisky. "Or that the warm waters of the Gulf Stream make this area ideal for the speedy maturation of single malt whisky?"

"Explains why so much of it was made here." Shannon tapped a finger on the text that stated the small island once boasted fifty illegal stills in the late eighteenth century. "And smuggled out of here, if the graphic is right."

Coleen suddenly stepped back. "Do you think that's Owen?" She tipped her head at a tall beanpole of a man who wore his hair buzzed close to his head and a well-trimmed goatee on his chin as he strode across the room.

"I hope so," Shannon said.

Coleen craned her neck. "I think his shirt says Owen."

Shannon squinted at the crisp black shirt he wore. When he moved closer, she read the distillery's name embroidered on one side in gold lettering and "Owen Reid" on the other.

"May I help you ladies?" His voice was free from the suspicion that had laced Holly's tone, giving Shannon a good vibe.

She introduced both of them and shook his hand. "We'd like to talk to you about Siobhan Paterson's recent death."

His large blue eyes filled with pain. "I didn't know Siobhan that well, so I'm not sure how I can help you."

"You and she weren't in a relationship?" Shannon asked.

He shook his head. "Not that I wouldn't have gladly started something up with her, but she was focused on her job until she could build her résumé. She wanted to break into the wedding-planning circuit in the big city." He shuddered. "Last thing I want is to live in the city, so we agreed to be friends and hung out occasionally."

"As far as you know, then, she didn't date anyone else?"

"No." A curious expression spread across his face. "Why'd you think we were in a relationship anyway?"

"Holly Taylor told us you were dating," Coleen blurted out.

"Holly Taylor." He crossed his arms and lifted his chin. "Don't believe a word she has to say. Especially when it comes to me. She had a crush on me in high school that I didn't return, and she's had nothing good to say about me ever since."

"Do you think she might have lied to us about anything else?" Shannon asked.

"Yeah. She's a little loony if you ask me. You know, like off the deep end. That's why Siobhan had her fired at the castle."

"How so?" Shannon asked.

"She propositioned a groom the night before his wedding. Can you believe that? She tried to deny it, but Siobhan witnessed her making her moves." He shook his head. "Worst part was, the groom took Holly up on it, and the bride and groom ended up calling off the wedding.

Siobhan was so disgusted, she made sure Holly was fired the next day."

"Exactly when did this happen?"

"Let's see." He tapped his chin with a long, square-tipped finger. "I was in an indoor tennis tournament that weekend, so it was three weekends ago."

Shannon wished she'd brought the bridal lists from the guestbook to see if a wedding occurred that weekend, but she'd left them on her bed. "I don't suppose Holly took the firing very well?"

"Hah! She was royally mad. Threatened to get even with Siobhan, and I have no doubt she tried to do so."

"Do you think she's capable of murder?" Coleen asked, excitement lifting her voice.

"Not only capable, but if I was the investigator on the case, she'd be my number-one suspect."

Shannon dug out her notebook and jotted down her phone number, then tore off the page and handed it to Owen. "Thank you for your time and honesty. If you think of anything else that might help us, give me a call anytime."

Owen folded the paper and shoved it in his shirt pocket. "Glad to help find Siobhan's killer. *And* get Holly off the streets so I don't have to worry about her anymore."

Shannon hurried out of the distillery, Coleen's feet pounding behind. Back in the van, Shannon turned to her friend. "Do you think he wanted Holly off the streets bad enough to lie, or was he telling the truth?"

"I watched him the whole time. If he was lying, he's very, very good at it."

"I thought the same thing."

"What do we do now?" Coleen asked.

"Let's go back to Holly's house. We need to ask her a few more questions."

"Sounds good." Coleen's face glowed with excitement as she cranked the engine and they zipped through town to Holly's house.

Shannon marched up to the door, knocked, and stood back, formulating her questions.

When no one answered, Coleen pushed closer and pounded on the door with both fists. "That ought to bring her to the door."

"No kidding. It was loud enough to wake the dead."

Coleen grinned. "We all have our talents. Mine is being loud."

"A truer statement has never been made." Shannon smiled at her friend and tapped her foot as she waited for Holly to answer.

"You're wasting your time," a gravelly female voice came from the yard next door. "She packed a bag and hightailed it out of here." The woman, in her late sixties, leaned on a broken spike of a washed-out picket fence between the properties. She wore a faded, flowery housecoat and had twined her hair around pink foam curlers.

Shannon picked her way through the weeds. By the time Shannon had reached the woman, she'd lit a cigarette and it dangled from her brightly painted lips.

"You saw Holly leave?" Shannon asked.

"She was toting a giant purple suitcase." The cigarette wobbled with each word. "Asked her where she was going, but as usual, she told me to mind my own business. And not in a nice way."

"Seems a shame to get yelled at when you were just being neighborly."

"Don't you know it?" She took a long drag of the cigarette and then stuck it in a charred crack in the fence. "The girl was a bit off her rocker and mean as all get-out, but I still tried to be kind to her."

Shannon nodded seriously. "I can tell you're a good neighbor."

Coleen snorted, and Shannon jabbed her in the side.

The woman's face turned suspicious. "She in trouble with the two of you?"

"We're with Hamilton Castle," Shannon said, exaggerating the truth. "And we wanted to talk to Holly about her employment there."

"Please." The woman smirked. "You're investigating the wedding planner's murder. I know because the inspector told me two ladies might come around asking questions and to keep what I know to myself."

Coleen crossed her arms. "He did, did he?"

"Don't worry. I never trust the law." She eyed Shannon. "You look decent enough." She glanced at Coleen and clucked.

Unsure what to make of her assessment of Coleen, Shannon rushed ahead. "Do you happen to know if Holly was home between five and seven on Monday morning?"

"Normally I could tell you about her comings and goings, but I spent the weekend at my daughter's house in Lamlash. Didn't get home until late Monday afternoon. But if you're thinking Holly mighta done in the wedding planner, I don't think you're off base. You should see the stuff she has posted on her walls."

"Stuff?" Coleen asked. "What stuff?"

"Take a look yourself," she said, coming out from behind the fence and heading toward Holly's window. "She never closes her curtains. Not even to change her clothes. Shocking, I tell you. Just shocking." She shook her head and gestured at the window.

Shannon started to tell the woman that peeping into someone's window was equally as shocking when she saw a picture of Siobhan with a red X scratched across her face. Shannon believed it to be a printed version of the same photo she'd seen on the castle website, depicting Siobhan standing next to a three-tier wedding cake.

"Check this out," Coleen said, dragging Shannon closer. "The other wall is filled with pictures of Owen." Coleen cupped her eyes and planted her forehead against the window. "There's one of Owen and Siobhan getting out of a car. Siobhan's face is gouged out." Coleen stood back. "She's clearly obsessed with him. And to think we talked to her just this morning. Right here. She could've ...."

Her words fell off, but her point was quite clear. Holly was unhinged, to say the least, and she could've hurt them. A queasy feeling roiled Shannon's stomach, and for once in her sleuthing career, she believed her foe was mentally unstable and required professional help. "We need to report this to the police."

The woman frowned. "I already told them she's a nutcase, and I know they talked to her."

"Did you specifically tell them about the pictures?"

"No, but they went in the house the other day when they talked to her, so they couldn't have missed them."

If Holly left the pictures up for their visit, Shannon thought. "We should be going. Thank you for your help." Shannon thought to give the woman her phone number, but she seemed a bit unhinged as well, and Shannon didn't want her to think she could call all the time.

"We're still going to report this to the police, aren't we?" Coleen whispered on the trip down the sidewalk.

"Absolutely." Shannon dug out her phone and, seeing all the signal bars filled for once, said, "I'll give Watson a call."

She dialed the inspector and waited for an answer. "Voice mail." She clicked off. "I'd leave a message, but who knows if my phone will work to take his call later? Beside, this is too urgent to let slide."

"To the police station, then?" Coleen asked.

"Yes." Shannon assessed her friend. "This is really bothering you."

"I've seen things like this on television and the movies, but it's a whole other thing to see it in person. Know what I mean?"

"Yes," Shannon said. "But the police will take care of Holly once we let them know about her."

In the small police station's parking lot, Shannon turned to Coleen. "Since you're a person of interest in this case, let me do all the talking. Not a peep, OK?" Coleen scowled. "Listen, sweetie, I know how hard it is for you not to say the first thing that comes to your mind, but I want them to take me seriously, and I doubt they'll do so if you chime in."

Coleen mimicked locking her lips and throwing away the key.

Shannon laughed. "You can talk on the way in."

Coleen pressed her lips together and shook her head. Shannon didn't know if she'd actually offended Coleen—something that was extremely hard to do—or if Coleen was simply taking the directions to the extreme.

Shannon walked up the ramp to the low-slung white building and held the door for her friend. She still had her lips pressed together, but an impish gleam brightened her face.

How long will she be able hold off speaking? Shannon wondered as she approached the uniformed officer at the front desk. "I've been looking into the Siobhan Paterson murder, and I have something urgent to report."

The woman sat back and appraised Shannon.

She tried her best to look honest, straightforward, and not as loony as the woman she was here to report. "I tried calling Inspector Watson, but he didn't answer, and I'm having a problem with cell service on the island, so I wanted to make sure someone in authority knows about the situation."

"Your name?" she asked.

"Shannon McClain."

She turned her penetrating gaze to Coleen. "And you?"

"Mm-mmm. Mmm-mm," Coleen said between closed lips.

Shannon shot Coleen an irritated glare. "She's Coleen Douglas. Her daughter is getting married at Hamilton Castle, and I'm a guest there as well."

The woman came to her feet. "Have a seat, and I'll see if PC Brodie or MacGregor has time to see you."

Shannon cringed at the mention of the same officers who'd escorted Coleen to the castle on Monday, but when the woman ran her gaze over Shannon, she forced out a smile. The minute she was out of sight, Shannon grabbed Coleen's arm. "No more funny business. This is serious, and we already have a strike against us with these officers."

Coleen mumbled something incoherent.

"I mean it, Coleen. What if they don't find Holly? What if she decides she doesn't like us looking into the murder, and she comes to the castle to do us in? Will you be so sassy then?"

Her expression fell. "Sorry. I was having a wee bit of fun, but it ends now."

"No, I'm the one who's sorry. I hate to be such a killjoy. But Holly is different from anybody I've ever dealt with. She scares me."

Coleen squeezed Shannon's arm. "Believe me, I get it. That wall was downright creepy."

Shannon heard footsteps coming their way before MacGregor poked his head around the corner. He approached warily. He didn't speak, instead looking at them like they were criminals recently apprehended from a crime spree in his community.

His look wouldn't deter Shannon. "I've come across a strong suspect in the death of Siobhan Paterson," she said. "She has a wall of pictures, including ones of Siobhan, in her home."

"Holly Taylor scratched out or drew an X through Siobhan's face in all of them." Coleen's tone asked him what he intended to do about it.

Wondering what made Coleen decide to talk, Shannon cast a questioning look at her.

Coleen shrugged, so Shannon continued. "We believe she's obsessed with Owen Reid, and she was jealous that he dated Siobhan."

MacGregor remained poker-faced. Though Shannon didn't want the emotional response she often got with Grayson, the silent treatment upset her more.

"Will you say something, for goodness' sake?" Coleen said. "This palace-guard routine isn't working."

He flinched and Shannon knew Coleen had pushed him too far. He opened his mouth, then closed it. Shannon braced herself for his irritation.

He fisted his hands. "I do believe Inspector Watson asked you ladies to leave the investigation to us."

Typical police response. One that Shannon didn't agree with. "That doesn't mean you should ignore any information we uncover."

He crossed his arms. "You're supposing this is new information to us."

"If it's not, why didn't you arrest Holly before she skipped town?" Attitude oozed from Coleen's words.

"Even if I wanted to answer that question," he said, arching an eyebrow, "I'm not at liberty to give you any details. So ... unless you have anything else for me, I have work to do."

Coleen opened and closed her mouth a few times as if searching for a comeback, but Shannon didn't bother thinking of one of her own. MacGregor didn't take kindly to their prying into the case, and she wasn't surprised. Still, they might need his help at some point during their stay, and she wouldn't walk away leaving them at odds with each other.

"I apologize if we've stepped on your toes," she said, infusing her voice with sincerity despite Coleen's mouth dropping open. "We do trust in you and the police force to perform a proper investigation, but we thought our information might be of help."

His shoulders relaxed. "I appreciate that, ma'am. I didn't mean to come across as unfriendly, but I have to think about your safety. I wouldn't want to encourage you to continue looking for a killer."

Shannon nodded, but honestly, no matter what the police told her, she wouldn't stop until she'd cleared Coleen's name and the murderer was behind bars.

— 12 —

Despite her queasy stomach after seeing Holly's wall of pictures, Shannon followed Coleen into the Country House. They found the Purls already seated at a round table near a roaring fire and crossed the packed dining room.

Betty lifted a teapot in greeting. "You two look cold. Have a seat by the fire, chase out the chill, and enjoy a warm cup of tea."

Shannon picked up a delicate teacup from the place setting next to Betty. Betty quickly filled it with a steaming liquid that Shannon's nose recognized as Earl Grey. "Perfect."

"Ooh, smoked salmon." Coleen pointed at the salads topped with fresh salmon sitting at each place setting as she slipped into her chair. "I hope no one minds if I start. Traipsing up and down the street wore me out."

Shannon wasn't sure how Coleen could be excited over food after their discovery at Holly's home, but maybe once Shannon relaxed with her friends, her appetite would make an appearance.

"That hill was quite a climb," Joyce said.

Coleen smiled and forked a bite of salmon. "We drove the van. I hope you haven't been waiting long."

"Not too long." Melanie's head popped up. "You made us climb the hill while you drove?"

"It wasn't intentional." Shannon set down her cup. "We

had to follow a lead, so it made sense to drive up here."

"What kind of lead?" Betty asked.

Shannon recapped their morning. "Holly certainly seems obsessed with Owen, and it's not hard to believe she killed Siobhan."

"It *is* hard to believe someone like that could live in such a quaint little town," Joyce said.

Shannon smiled at her friend and opted to change to a positive focus. "So you enjoyed your morning here, then?"

"It was perfect." Joyce smiled. "In fact, I'd love to come back tomorrow. We didn't get through half the shops, and I for one have not had my fill of the charming village."

"I thought we were spending the day preparing for the show of presents." Kate, the only never-married woman in the group, would be the one to mention the Scottish tradition. The Purls had discussed the tradition, which was much like bridal showers in America, at great length before their trip, so they knew what to expect.

Coleen swallowed her bite of salad. "That won't take all day, and like I said before, you need to have some fun while you're here."

"Speaking of fun." Melanie turned to Shannon. "Stitches has the most amazing assortment of Shetland wool. We even picked up a few skeins to tide you over on the trip home."

"Thanks for thinking of me." Shannon laughed. "Or did you do it in self-defense so I'll keep busy and won't chat all the way home?"

Melanie waved a hand. "Doesn't matter what you do. I plan to live life to the fullest while I'm here and sleep on the way back."

"Then tomorrow I insist that you all return to the village before the sightseeing trip I planned. But now ..." Coleen forked another bite of salmon to her mouth and moaned. "So good."

Shannon dug into her salad too, and soon the waitress was at their table, serving the main course.

"Welcome, ladies," she said to Shannon and Coleen as she set a plate in front of Betty. "Today we're serving roast breast of duck stuffed with wild rice, walnuts, and raspberries. It's served with a rich port-wine glaze and potatoes baked with cream and garlic."

Shannon could feel the pounds being added on her hips just at the description of the food, but once the plate was set in front of her, she couldn't resist. Like the other ladies, she didn't come up for conversation until she'd sampled the meal several times.

Coleen opened her mouth to say something, but her face suddenly paled, and she stared openmouthed at the door. Shannon followed her gaze and found Inspector Watson standing by the hostess station, his eyes searching the room like a heat-seeking missile. The moment he locked on Coleen, his gangly legs set in motion, and he wound his way through the other tables.

"I'm sorry to interrupt, Mrs. Douglas," he said to Coleen, though he didn't sound sorry at all. "But I need a word in private."

Coleen cast a plea-filled glance at Shannon, who quickly joined her friend. "There aren't any diners near the kitchen door," Shannon said. "Let's chat over there."

Watson pursed his lips in a sour expression but nodded and stood back.

"What do you think he wants?" Coleen whispered frantically.

"No idea, but remember, no matter what he says or asks, you're innocent, and that will all come out in the end."

Coleen gave a firm nod. "You are so right. I *am* innocent, and nothing he can say or do will bring down my mood." Near the door, she spun and crossed her arms in her bulldog fighting stance. Shannon loved to see Coleen had quickly replaced her shock with determination. "What can I do for you, Inspector?"

"We've confirmed Siobhan's embezzlement, giving you a prime motive for wanting to end her life. Coupled with the other evidence, this makes you a definite suspect."

Coleen's confidence quickly fled. As she tried to respond to his accusation, she sputtered like a deflating balloon.

"I'm assuming you have proof of the embezzlement from *Coleen's* account and not from some other wedding," Shannon said as she grasped Coleen's shoulder in solidarity.

Coleen must have felt Shannon's strength through her touch, because she jerked back her shoulders and eyed Watson. "Yes. I'd like to see some proof."

Watson pulled a large envelope from his breast pocket and unfolded a sheaf of papers. "I need you to verify these charges for your daughter's wedding." He handed the papers to Coleen.

Shannon looked over her friend's shoulder at invoices for castle guest rooms, the chapel charge, and the projected expenses for the reception.

Coleen flipped to the last page and then looked up. "I can't be certain these numbers are exact, but the amount is in the ballpark of what we paid."

Watson gave her another set of invoices. "Now take a look at these."

Coleen quickly skimmed through invoices for the same vendors, but not too quickly for Shannon to see the numbers were considerably lower.

"So Siobhan *was* padding my bills and pocketing the difference," Coleen said.

"I'm afraid so."

Shannon wasn't quite as eager to embrace the obvious. "How do you know one set of invoices isn't from earlier and then was revised as the costs rose?"

"Our forensic accountant reviewed the books and confirmed that the amounts listed on the second set of invoices are the same as those entered in the castle's hospitality account."

If only Watson had been forthcoming about his plan to have an accountant look at the books, Shannon wouldn't have wasted time scanning the invoices that morning and sending them to Michael. Plus now Michael was reviewing them and wasting his time as well.

Shannon opened her mouth to ask for additional details.

Before she could speak, Watson lifted his hand like a stop sign. "Before you ask, we tracked the money and proved it had been moved out of the castle's accounts."

"How?" Shannon asked.

"Checks were issued to a bogus company."

"A bogus company," Coleen said. "I don't understand."

"Siobhan couldn't simply withdraw the money without an invoice to cover her tracks. Nor could she write a check to herself without leaving a trail. Instead, she created a fictitious company, rented a post-office box, and had the checks delivered there."

Shannon had to give Siobhan credit for her imagination. "How do you know she created this company? Couldn't someone else at the castle do so?"

"First, castle management accounts and wedding accounts are kept separate. Siobhan and the owners were the only ones who could access the wedding accounts. Second, the entries were created under her login for the financial software."

"I'm sure you also reviewed Siobhan's bank accounts," Shannon said. "Did you find the money deposited there?"

He shook his head.

Just as Shannon suspected. Watson didn't have enough proof, but he'd presented it to Coleen in hopes that she would confess, and Shannon wasn't going to let him get away with it. "I may be an amateur sleuth, but even I know that someone could steal Siobhan's login information. Unless you can prove the missing money made it to Siobhan's account, you don't have concrete proof of embezzlement."

Watson's expression soured as he pulled his cap from his pocket. "It's simply a matter of time before we find the money, at which point we will have another conversation." He strode away without his usual pleasant goodbye.

Coleen spun on Shannon. "You were amazing. Thank you."

Shannon smiled, but in her heart, she knew Watson and his team would find the money, and then the conversation *would* take a different path. "Let's get back to that wonderful duck and our friends."

They rejoined the Purls, and while Coleen filled the ladies in about Watson, Shannon texted Michael and told him not to spend any time on the invoices.

"You should have seen Shannon," Coleen exclaimed. "She knew exactly what to say to the inspector to keep him at bay." She lifted her teacup. "A toast to the best friend a person could have."

Shannon wished Coleen wouldn't make such a fuss, but her friend did everything with gusto. Shannon knew better than to try to stop her, so she sat back and listened to the fine china clinking.

Coleen didn't quit gushing until their server arrived. She carried lingonberry tarts served with homemade cassis ice cream.

Melanie shivered as a plate was set in front of her. "Not sure I can eat ice cream on such a cold day."

The waitress winked at Melanie. "I dare you to try a bite and not finish it."

"You're on." Melanie laughed and dug into the ice cream. She put the first bite in her mouth and moaned, her eyes rolling back. "Simply amazing. For once I'm glad to be wrong." She took a second taste, and the others joined her.

Silence reigned as they quickly consumed the sweet yet tart dessert.

Betty sat back and patted her stomach. "We won't fit in our seat belts on the plane if we keep eating this way."

"We can walk it off this afternoon on a hike I have planned," Shannon said as the last utensil clanked to the plate. "My favorite trail that I used to take with my father will lead us to the loch where we're sure to see seals and otters. And we might spot a golden eagle or two on the way."

"Sounds wonderful." Joyce pushed back her chair and they all filed outside.

They found Watson standing next to the door, his phone pressed to his ear. He excused himself from his caller. "Mrs. Douglas. A word?"

Coleen and Shannon both stepped over to him.

"Forensics confirmed your prints were found on the box for the missing wine stopper."

Emotions raced across Coleen's face, but in the end, she controlled them. "That's not unexpected. I told you I touched it."

"It's one thing to expect the results. Another to actually receive them." Watson fixed a sharp stare on Coleen that would have made Shannon cringe, but Coleen held her own, her expression filled with feistiness. "I remind you again, Mrs. Douglas, not to leave the area. I'd get awful cranky if I had to come looking for you when I'm ready to make an arrest."

— 13 —

Back at the castle, Shannon listened to the rain pick up, whipping with ferocity against the stained glass windows on the stairway landing. Not surprising, as December was the rainiest month of the year, but the inclement weather dashed her hopes of heading up to the hill to call the brides. She shed her jacket and draped it over her arm.

She caught sight of the castle brochures on the table in the grand hall below, which gave her an idea. She jogged down the stairs and grabbed a brochure containing a map of the estate and the castle's floor plan. She hadn't explored the entire castle, so maybe there was another spot where she could get cell reception.

She heard Coleen and Gemma's voices coming from down the hall, and, hoping Coleen would join her, Shannon reversed course. She found them outside Coleen's room. Gemma's eyes were watery and red, and she clutched a lace handkerchief. Another bridal meltdown, Shannon supposed. Perhaps she could help.

"Everything all right?" she asked.

Gemma's crying picked up speed.

Coleen looked frazzled. "We've had a problem with the flowers. Gemma has her heart set on calla lilies, but Siobhan didn't order them, and now the supplier can't get them shipped in time."

Shannon laid a comforting hand on Gemma's shoulder.

"I'm sorry, sweetie. I know how hard all these setbacks must be for you, but you can find a substitute equally as stunning."

Gemma sobbed wildly and flung herself into Shannon's arms. Shannon looked over Gemma's shoulder at Coleen, who mouthed, "Sorry."

Gemma pulled back. "Thank you for being so understanding." She looked at Coleen. "That's what I needed, Mum. Not a lecture on how in the scheme of life, not having calla lilies is no big deal."

"But I ..." Coleen let her voice fall off like she hadn't the strength to go on.

Shannon smiled at Gemma. "Maybe a nice soak in that amazing claw-foot tub in your room would help."

Gemma nodded. "Just what I need."

As Gemma walked away, Coleen sighed deeply.

"Hey, it will be all right," Shannon said. "You know a mother's words are often taken the wrong way and then someone else says the exact same thing and it makes sense."

"Aye, but I've had a bit too much of it this week, and I'm getting a headache." Coleen did a few neck rolls.

"What you need is a diversion from the wedding. I was on my way to explore the castle and see if I can find a spot inside to make phone calls. You should join me."

"Fiona says the only consistent spot is up on the hill."

Right now, Shannon didn't care if she located a cell signal. Taking a walk with her friend would get Coleen's mind off Gemma. "Let's explore the place for fun, then. It will refresh you, and you'll be able to go on."

"Brilliant."

"Can I put my jacket in your room?"

"I'll do it."

Coleen took the coat to her room, and Shannon studied the brochure. She'd visited most areas of the castle except the former dungeon. It served as a sitting area where Fiona also displayed her paintings. Being more familiar with Fiona's work could help Shannon gain Fiona's cooperation in the investigation, so a visit could serve two purposes.

Coleen returned, her expression already less tense. "Where to?"

"The dungeon," Shannon said with a fiendish tone.

Coleen grinned. "The perfect room for my mood right now."

"Remember, all this drama will be over in a few days."

Coleen's brow furrowed.

"What did I say?"

"That also means I'm losing my baby in a few days."

"Ah, I feel your pain," Shannon said and meant every word.

"I know I'm being irrational," Coleen continued. "Gemma's been out of the house for years now, but there's something so permanent about her getting married."

"Keep remembering she's marrying a wonderful young man. Maybe that will help." Shannon held out her phone to watch the signal indicator as they worked their way down a labyrinth of hallways. She stopped in front of a doorway with a heavy iron gate as a door. The lowest bar on her phone lit up. "I have a bit of a signal here, which seems odd, given all the stone surrounding us."

"I'll never understand how those things work."

"The list is in my jacket. I'll have to go get it and come back." Shannon pocketed her phone. "But first, I want to take a look at Fiona's paintings so I have something to

talk to her about if I need to ask her for another favor."
Shannon peered into the dim light cast by an ancient wall
sconce at the steep stone stairs heading into the basement.
"This must be the dungeon."

"It is. Fiona gave me a tour the first day I was here."
Coleen shuddered. "Are you sure you want to go down there?"

"Sure. Why not?"

Coleen shrugged. "I guess being locked in the staircase is
still bothering me. So humor me, OK? Let's at least tell someone
where we are in case the gate gets locked behind us."

Though Shannon doubted such a thing would happen
again, she wanted to make Coleen feel comfortable, so
she pulled out her phone. "I'll send a text to the Purls."
Thankful she'd upgraded to an international plan for
the trip, Shannon fired off the text. "Done. If we don't
come back, maybe one of them will have a signal and get
the text."

She pulled open the door, the rusty hinges rasping over
the pin.

Coleen shuddered again.

"Relax," Shannon said. "I'm guessing they didn't grease
the hinges to make the atmosphere scarier."

Shannon started down the stairs, but despite her brave
words to Coleen, memories of the brief time locked in the
secret stairwell sent a shiver over her back. When they
reached a narrow landing, they turned toward a catacomb
of cells, all with the same iron doors securing the spaces. In
the center chamber, the ceiling rose, making it feel like they
were at the bottom of a well, looking up.

Coleen ran her hand over deep gouges in the walls.

"Fiona told me these marks are from lowering prisoners down on a rope."

Shannon suddenly wished she were anywhere but here, but when she took a step to leave, a sensor activated the lights, flooding the space with a warm glow and easing her apprehensions. Lights came alive over the paintings, illuminating large oil canvases.

Shannon entered the first cell. The lights flickered briefly.

Coleen grabbed Shannon's arm. "What if we lose power from the storm? We should've been prepared with a flashlight."

"We can always use the flashlight on my phone." Shannon stepped closer to four landscape paintings with an aged appearance. A placard with the painting's title and original artist's name as well as a photograph hung next to each one. "These look old. Are you sure Fiona painted all of these?"

"Yes. She's studied all the masters, and apparently, she can mimic their work so well only experts can tell the difference. That's how they came to live at the castle. The owners wanted to provide a realistic setting for their guests, but they didn't want to display original artwork, so they commissioned her to copy them."

"Amazing." Shannon moved from room to room, impressed with the different techniques Fiona employed to make the paintings resemble the masters Shannon had studied in her college art classes. "It's hard to believe she did all these."

"I know, right? I even said that to her."

"You didn't!" Shannon flashed a reproachful look at her friend.

Coleen's face took on a sheepish look. "I didn't think before it came out. She took offense to it, so she insisted on showing me the current painting she was working on." Coleen looked at her watch. "Each day—around this time, actually—she drags me to her studio. She must think showing me the progress on the painting proves she's actually doing it."

"You still sound doubtful."

"Well, I've never seen her paint. I did overhear her talking to Greer about one she'd recently completed called *Landscape at Coubron* by an artist named Corot. I don't think she'd lie to Greer, but for all I know, she had little elves in her studio paint that one."

"There are no elves." Fiona descended the stairs. She wore ballet flats that muffled her approach, and Shannon had no idea how long she'd been listening to their conversation. "Come. I will paint in front of you."

"That's not necessary," Coleen said. "I was kidding."

"My work is not a joke." She gestured at the stairs. "Come."

Shannon knew better than to argue with a temperamental artist. But she doubted Coleen would be compliant, so she took her arm and led her up the stairs.

"She seems miffed at me," Coleen whispered.

"You offended her by doubting her skills, and now you'll have to watch her paint."

"You're coming with me."

"*I* wasn't the one who insulted her." When Shannon stepped into the hallway, her phone rang and she eagerly dug it out. "It's Michael. Since we don't know if there will be cell reception in Fiona's studio, I'll have to take this here."

"Of course," Coleen said, her tone now most agreeable. "A call from Michael will get you excused from anything I might want you to do." She ended with a wink.

Shannon rolled her eyes and stepped into a secluded alcove for her conversation.

"You will stay with me while I paint." Fiona clamped a hand on Coleen's arm and tugged her down the hallway.

Shannon clicked Talk on her phone. "Hello, Michael."

"Good," he said. "I'm glad the call got through to you."

The urgency in his voice set her on edge. "Is something wrong?"

"Wrong? No. I simply wanted to check in to see if Coleen's prints turned up on the murder weapon after all."

"The police haven't found the stopper yet, but they confirmed her prints on the box. The inspector warned her that an arrest was imminent, but he didn't actually arrest her." *Yet*, Shannon thought but didn't want to put voice to it.

"That's good news. He must have some doubt about her guilt."

"I hope so, because I'm not making much progress on my end of the investigation." She told him about her day and her recent attempt to find cell reception in the castle.

"I'd be happy to call the brides. If you'd like me to," he quickly added.

"Coleen told me I should ask you to do it."

He didn't respond for a few moments, the silence heavy and uncomfortable. "Sounds like you don't think it's a good idea."

"I don't want to impose on you. You've been a good friend."

"No imposition," he said. "I'm glad to help."

Shannon had hoped he'd comment on her use of the word *friend* to clarify where they stood with each other, but it wasn't like Michael to share his feelings with her. "I'll email the list to you then."

"Perfect. I'll jump on it the minute I get it." He paused. "But why did you say to ignore the financial records you sent?"

"Inspector Watson had a forensic accountant review the records, and they proved someone was embezzling from the wedding accounts by using bogus vendors. He has yet to connect it to Siobhan's private accounts, but I suspect he will. And that legitimizes Coleen's motive for wanting to kill Siobhan."

"Now that's an area I can help you with," he said excitedly. "I'll get my team looking for any accounts that Siobhan might have hidden."

"You're already doing so much to help," she protested. "I hate to monopolize your time."

"No problem. It would help my team find the info if you can get access to the accounts that prove embezzlement. Is that something you can do?"

"I'll talk with the caretakers, but they were good friends with Siobhan, and they don't want to give out any information that might sully her reputation."

"You can be pretty persuasive when you put your mind to it. At least with me." He fell silent, and she wondered if he thought her influence was a good thing or a bad thing. She'd opened her mouth to ask when he continued, "Other than the murder, how's the rest of your trip going?"

The dungeon door shifted and creaked, grabbing Shannon's attention. "I have a love-hate relationship with this castle. It's very interesting to explore, and yet it's kind of creepy."

"Creepy how?"

"Coleen and I got trapped in a secret stairwell the other day." She gave an abbreviated version of the incident. "It may have been a miscommunication with the staff, but I don't think so."

He blew out a breath. "I don't like the sound of this. You need to keep your head on a swivel. Stay with the group."

Shannon searched for a way to respond to his comment. Since she was alone in a remote part of the castle, she could hardly say she'd taken precautions and remained with her friends.

"You're alone now, aren't you?" he asked.

"Yes," she replied, both hating and loving the fact that he could read her so well.

"Where?" His one word, short and clipped, revealed his ongoing anxiety from losing his wife to a drug dealer seeking revenge.

"I'm standing outside the dungeon," she admitted reluctantly.

"The dungeon? Why on earth are you there? *Especially* on your own."

"Coleen was with me, but the castle caretaker dragged Coleen off to watch while she painted."

"Am I missing something here, or does this caretaker do something different when painting a wall, making it a sight to see?"

Shannon chuckled. "Fiona's painting a picture, not a wall. Coleen questioned whether Fiona actually completed a replica of a painting. I think Coleen said it was *Landscape at Coubron* by an artist named Corot or something like that.

Anyway, Fiona overheard Coleen's comment and wanted to prove to Coleen that she knows how to paint."

"She sounds like a temperamental artist." He paused for a long moment. "Will you please go join them so you're not alone?"

"I should rescue Coleen anyway since I'm partially to blame for getting her busted."

"Stay on the phone with me until you get there, OK?"

His concern touched her. "OK, but I warn you, I'm sure to lose reception as soon as I move."

"I'll take the chance. But in case I do lose you, remember to email the list of brides to me so I can make the calls right away."

"You actually want the list that fast, or do you want to know I've made it back to my room?" she asked, proving she was getting to know him as well as he was her.

"Both."

"I'll head to my room first and can have the list to you in five minutes, assuming the storm hasn't taken out the Internet."

"Storm? You didn't mention a storm." He paused and the line hissed with interference. "You shouldn't be alone. The power could go out."

He was right, and she probably should've stayed with Coleen. She started down the darkened hallway and the wall sconces flickered again. Her phone crackled.

"Are you still there?" she asked.

A garbled response filtered through the phone. Then the line went dead. She looked at the screen—zero bars. The same disconcerting feeling settled over her as last night when she'd heard the cellar noises. She quickened her steps and continued to sweep the area for any sign of danger. She wouldn't be caught unaware again; the consequences could be deadly.

— 14 —

Visions of Holly's disturbing wall of pictures kept sleep at bay, and Shannon finally gave up. With everyone in bed, she didn't want to traipse around the castle alone, but she couldn't lie awake and think about Holly any longer. Maybe a few turns up and down the hallway would clear her mind and tire her enough to sleep.

She climbed from the downy-soft bed and dressed quickly. Shadows from the dim wall sconce cloaked the stairway, upping her anxiety. She was glad she'd decided not to descend the main staircase to the depths that darkness cast.

She set off down the hallway and kept up a rapid pace. Out of the corner of her eye, she caught a flash of light through the window facing the ocean. Another flash out at sea split the darkness before it quickly disappeared.

She stopped and watched. Nothing. Then a flash again, like an approaching boat that was bobbing in and out of view. Who would be out in a boat in the middle of the night?

Holly? The killer? Or were they one and the same?

"Stop it, Shannon," she mumbled to herself. She'd let her unease over Holly fuel her imagination.

She started walking again, glancing every so often out the window and not catching sight of the boat. She walked and pumped her arms until her breathing grew labored, and she halted to catch her breath.

A light flashed on the beach ... a small prick of light, like someone had extinguished a flashlight.

She hadn't imagined it. Someone was out there. But who would be on the beach so late at night, and why?

Another flash lit the darkness. This one was longer, like the sweep of a flashlight measuring the beach for safety.

Her heart rate kicked up, but it had nothing to do with the exercise. Should she check it out or go to her room? Could she even get down to the beach from the castle grounds? Common sense said go to her room and lock the door. Her sleuthing sense said check it out—and her sleuthing sense always won.

She made a quick trip back to her bedroom to grab her cellphone for light. Back on the landing, she realized she had seen two separate lights, and they moved steadily closer until she could vaguely make out two figures, each holding a light and easing their way across the beach toward the bluff.

They headed straight for the castle. But could they climb the rugged bluff she'd seen on her walk to Siobhan's cottage the other day?

The arcs grew closer, then disappeared. The hillside hid them from her view, or they'd turned off their flashlights. They surely wouldn't try to climb the hill with their lights off, so it made more sense that she just couldn't see them any longer.

Uncertain about how to proceed, she opted to wait.

The grandfather clock below her beat a steady rhythm. *Tick. Tick. Tick.* It counted the time that felt endless as her pulse raced ahead.

Time slipped by. Five, maybe ten minutes. Nothing. She had to check it out.

She eased down the stairs. Slowly. One step at a time until she reached the grand hall. A single wall sconce lit the cavernous space. She wanted to illuminate the room with the flashlight on her cell, but she didn't want to give herself away if someone was watching.

At the main window overlooking the bluff, she peeked out. The moon had slipped behind heavy clouds, and darkness gathered on the lawn. She waited. Watching. Hoping to see where the light bearers were lurking. Nothing. A better view could be had from the library.

She backed away and followed the wall to the wide, wood-encased arch. Her fingers found the smooth wood, and she slipped around the corner. Darker here, it raised her apprehension to an all-time high.

Breathe, she warned herself, *before you become light-headed. In. Out. In. Out. Nice and deep.*

A loud thump sounded from the cellar, and she jumped. Had someone entered the castle through the cellar? Was there even an entrance down there?

She reversed course toward the kitchen, her sneaker-clad feet finding their way silently over the stone floor. She moved on. Inch by inch. Listening. Breathing. Waiting for another sound to direct her.

There. In the distance below. A dragging noise. Someone pulling a heavy object across stone. Scraping. Grinding. Grating.

She reached the kitchen. With the space as dark as the other night, she felt her way to the cellar door.

She heard voices now. Low-pitched. Muffled. She wasn't sure if it was a man or woman or both.

Was Greer fixing a problem again? Odds were against it.

So who was down there—and why?

The voices suddenly moved away from her, fading and then disappearing under the floor. Heading toward an outside exit? Maybe. She needed to get back to the main window in the grand hall.

As she turned and fled, her knee slammed into a heavy oak chair. She bit her lip to keep from crying out. Faster now, she moved through the darkness and into the muted light of the grand hall.

At the window, she slipped behind the heavy velvet drapes and watched. Flashlights moved on the beach again. The opposite direction this time. Heading for a boat? Likely. Someone had come and gone. Who? The killer?

A sudden movement by Coleen's van drew Shannon's focus from the beach. Another person scurried around the car. Hurried, quick movements at first, then gracefully easing alongside the vehicle.

A woman? The fluid movements indicated as much.

Holly?

Shannon couldn't let her get away. She searched the room for a weapon. Spotting a rack by the door filled with large umbrellas, she grabbed one and flipped on the outside light as she simultaneously swung the door open. The light spilled onto a person dressed in black as she spray-painted a message on the far side of Coleen's van.

Shannon burst outside. The cold slapped her face, and she gasped but kept going. "Stop! I've called the police."

The woman didn't look up or look back, but tossed the can and fled down the drive. Shannon gave chase, but the woman was small, wiry, and quick. She darted into the ditch and disappeared. Shannon could continue after her, but she'd never catch her. Besides, what would she do if she did? If the woman was Holly, she could be armed.

Moments later, a car engine roared to life, then squealing tires broke through the night and Shannon caught a glimpse of a red vehicle as it sped away. The vandal had obviously stashed a car or stolen one to make her getaway.

Shannon held out her phone and moved around until she found a signal, weak but strong enough to summon the police. She started to dial 911, then remembered the emergency number in Scotland was 999. She pressed the digits, and as she waited for an answer, she kept sweeping the darkness with her gaze.

When the operator answered, Shannon barely let him get out his greeting before she blurted out, "I caught someone vandalizing my friend's car. I chased after her, but I couldn't catch her. Then I heard a car start, it looked red as it sped away."

"Are you someplace safe?"

Shannon peered into the darkness again. "Maybe I should go back inside." *And lock the door.*

"Definitely."

The operator gathered her information, including her location.

"I've dispatched an officer from Lamlash," he said, his voice starting to break up. "But it will take some time for him to arrive. Would you like to remain on the line with me until the officer arrives?"

"I can't get a signal inside the castle, so I'll hang up now."

"Stay inside, ma'am. Call back if you have any other problems."

Shannon closed and locked the door, resting her back

against it for added measure. A movement to the right caught her eye and spiked her pulse. She raised the umbrella high until Greer and Fiona, both looking sleepy, stepped into the hall. A breath of relief slipped from Shannon's lips.

"We heard the shouting." Greer crossed the room. "Is everything all right?"

Shannon nodded and wasn't surprised to see how much her hands trembled as she stowed her phone in her pocket.

"What's going on, Mrs. McClain?" Greer scrubbed his hand over his face.

"I couldn't sleep. I saw a boat approaching the beach and then flashlights as two people walked toward the cliff. Then I heard noises in the cellar. And voices."

"Not unusual," Fiona said. "Our guests often let the lore of the castle get their imaginations going."

After the false alarm the night before, Shannon could see how they thought she was making this up. "I know what I heard. Besides, I also saw a woman spray-painting Coleen's car. I chased her down the driveway, but she got away."

Greer cast a worried look at Fiona, and she slipped under his arm.

"I've already phoned 999," Shannon said, hoping to ease their concern. "An officer is on his way from Lamlash."

Greer scowled. "Great. He'll likely arrive, lights and sirens blaring, disturbing the other guests."

Fiona peered up at her husband. "I might as well put tea on and prepare a light snack."

"I'll help you, my love."

Shannon's mouth fell open. "I don't believe you two. Someone vandalized Coleen's car, and you're going to make snacks?"

"Aye, that we are," Greer said. "Tonight isn't the first time a vandal has wanted to spoil things around here, and our guests always come first."

"Come sit by the fireplace." Fiona took Shannon's arm. "Greer will get a fire burning in no time, and I'll bring you a cuppa."

Shannon would have rather gone back outside for a good look at what the woman had painted on the van, but she'd see it when the police arrived. She let Fiona lead her to a wingback chair by the fireplace where Greer was already kneeling on the wide stone hearth.

"We always lay the fire the night before, so it will be ablaze in a moment." He struck a match. Dried kindling snapped and crackled as it caught and flared into an orange flame, casting light into corners that had felt so foreboding a moment ago.

"I'll be right back with the tea." Fiona turned on several lamps on her way to the hallway.

In the distance, Shannon heard a siren and wished the officer would turn it off before approaching and waking the Purls, Coleen, and her daughters. Shannon sat back, watching the flames dance in the fireplace while the siren wound steadily closer. The narrow road to the castle paralleled the winding coastline, edging dangerously along the cliffs. She doubted the officer could be racing along at high speeds.

As the wail grew uncomfortably near, Fiona reappeared carrying a silver tray with a delicate teapot, several fragile cups, and a plate laden with cookies. Blue lights twisted through the window and reflected from the polished tray.

Fiona set it on a gleaming mahogany table near Shannon. "Greer," she said, "please hurry out to the officer and get him to turn off that blasted siren."

As Greer exited, a cold chill whisked across the room and made the fire dance wildly. Shannon got up, not to pour the tea but to go outside and talk to the officer. As she reached the door, the siren stilled and the blue lights stopped. She pulled open the front door, and as she stepped outside, Greer returned with PC MacGregor in tow.

"Och, go back inside, Mrs. McClain," Greer said. "Mac-Gregor will have a spot of tea with you and take your statement."

"Ma'am," MacGregor said before he tromped past her and into the castle.

She often forgot how laid-back Scottish folks in the country could be. So as not to seem adversarial, she complied and crossed the room. MacGregor held the fragile teapot's handle between his thick paws and looked extremely uncomfortable with such fine china.

"Let me help." Shannon stifled a grin and took the pot from him.

"These frilly little tea doodads are a bit much for me," he admitted.

"Let me get you a stout mug, my friend," Greer offered.

"I wouldn't say no to that." MacGregor smiled for the first time, and Shannon found him to be quite a pleasant-looking man when he wasn't scowling.

"Let's get right to it." He sat in the chair Shannon had vacated and pulled out a notepad. "Tell me exactly what happened tonight. No embellishments necessary."

Shannon had opened her mouth to speak when Coleen,

dressed in a fluffy blue robe, bustled into the room. "And what are you up to now, Shannon? The sirens were enough to scare my hair straight."

"Come have some tea, and you can hear my story while I share it with Officer MacGregor."

MacGregor looked less than enthused to have Coleen join them, but he appeared very irritated when the Purls, en masse, descended the stairs.

"Guess we'll be needing more cups," Greer said from the entrance to the room. He gave MacGregor a handcrafted stone mug glazed in a deep blue.

"One of your own creations?" MacGregor asked, holding up the mug.

"Aye," Greer said as he left the room.

"What's going on?" Betty asked.

"We had a little incident. I'm about to tell Officer MacGregor about it. Grab some tea if you like and settle in."

"No tea for me." Kate, wearing a fluffy pink robe with white poodles embroidered on it and heavy flannel pajamas, eyed the cookies before passing them by and curling into a chair.

"Always have to sample the baked goods." Joyce grabbed a few cookies and sat on the sofa next to Betty.

Melanie filled the last two cups with tea, then added a heavy dose of cream, as did Coleen, while they chatted about the rude awakening.

"I do have other things to do, so …," MacGregor said pointedly as he tapped his watch.

Shannon didn't want to tell her story again, so she waited for Melanie and Coleen to sit and pay attention. "It all started when I couldn't sleep."

"Again?" Coleen asked.

"You poor thing," Joyce said. "Do you have anything you can take? My doctor gave me a prescription in case I had difficulty with jet lag, but I wouldn't feel right about sharing it with you."

"Of course you wouldn't," Coleen said. "It's illegal, and PC MacGregor here would arrest you if you did."

Joyce clutched the chest of her silvery robe. "Oh, my, you're right."

"Maybe you could see the local doctor in the morning," Kate suggested.

MacGregor sighed. "Your story, Mrs. McClain. Can we please get to your story?"

MacGregor had irritated Shannon earlier today, but the chatty Purls were more than making up for that. She stifled a smile before resuming her story. "I decided to take a walk to tire myself out. That's when I saw a boat approaching the beach, followed by someone walking on the beach, holding flashlights."

"I doubt there was a boat at this time of night," MacGregor said. "There's a lighted buoy out in the harbor. Maybe that's what you saw."

"My thoughts exactly." Greer joined them with a tray holding cups and another assortment of cookies.

Betty jumped up. "Ooh, yum. More to taste."

"Bring me a chocolate one," Kate said, caving in to the desire she always worked so hard to resist.

MacGregor stood and glared down on them. "If the lot of you don't pipe down, I'll be forced to take Mrs. McClain down to the station to get her statement."

"Oh, sorry," Joyce said, then looked at Kate. "One or two, hon?"

"One, please."

MacGregor groaned.

"Anyway," Shannon said, rushing on, "after that, I heard a noise in the cellar. Like someone was dragging something across the floor. Then voices."

"Our furnace makes quite a racket," Greer offered. "And you know how the air in these old places often sounds like whispering."

"Likely the case." MacGregor jotted something on his notepad.

Shannon's frustration flared at their dismissal, but she didn't want to argue, so she moved on. "When the voices faded, I looked out the window again and saw the flashlights on the beach. This time they were moving back toward the boat."

"The boat you didn't actually see," MacGregor clarified.

Shannon chose not to respond to his comment and moved on. "My attention was immediately drawn to someone moving around Coleen's van."

"Oh dear." Coleen spoke up. "Do you think it's OK? It's a rental, you know. Of course, our car insurance applies, but you know what a hassle dealing with something like that can be. I'd rather not—"

"The statement." MacGregor had clearly reached the end of his rope with them.

"I turned on the outside light and saw a woman dressed in black from head to toe." Shannon looked at Coleen. "Sorry, Coleen, but she spray-painted something on the side of the van."

"Oh no," Coleen said.

"What did she paint?" Melanie asked excitedly.

"I don't know," Shannon said. "I was too far away to see it. When the woman took off, I chased after her. I couldn't catch up, but I heard a car start up and tires squeal away, so I called the police."

MacGregor set his mug on the table and then stood. "Let's take a look at it, shall we?"

Shannon led the way to the door and heard MacGregor's big boots tromping behind her as well as the scuffle of several pairs of slippers. She didn't have to turn to think about what a sight they all made in their robes, pajamas, and slippers. Nor did she have to look to imagine the expression on MacGregor's face when they accompanied him.

Steeling herself for the sight ahead, Shannon circled the van. Bold, roughly scrawled black letters spelled out a message.

"Stop meddling."

"Guess we've hit a nerve," Coleen whispered from behind.

"I guess we did," Shannon replied. "Question is, whose nerve did we hit?"

— 15 —

The next morning, Shannon closed the latest email from Michael. He'd had no luck in finding Siobhan's secret bank account, but he had located two brides who mentioned irregularities in their wedding finances. He asked Shannon to call him the minute she got his email, even if it was the middle of the night his time, which it was.

Should she actually phone him and wake him up? She had to if she wanted to clear Coleen's name. Plus, he wouldn't have told her to call if he didn't think it was important.

Guilt peppering her, Shannon grabbed her coat and made a quick stop in Fiona's office. Yesterday, Fiona had agreed to ask the castle owners if Shannon could look at the books. Fiona said she should have an answer today, and Shannon wanted to follow up before her day began. Finding the office vacant, she jotted a quick message on a sticky note and placed it on the computer monitor. Her fingers itched to wake up the computer to see if she could glean valuable information, but that would take her research a step further than her ethics would allow.

She slipped into her coat and headed up the hill for cell reception. Coleen's vandalized van sat in the same location, the roughly scrawled message reminding Shannon of the previous night's horror. She tucked her coat around her body as if it could provide some safety. The police had arrived at sunrise to process the scene in the light of day.

They'd scoured every inch around the van and followed the vandal's trail, but found few leads. Or so they said. The tight-lipped MacGregor didn't offer any details about the scene, and his blank expression gave nothing away.

Shivering, Shannon had tucked her head down and had started into the brisk wind when Coleen's voice came from behind. "Wait up."

Shannon turned to watch her friend pump her fists as she nearly jogged to catch up. She wore a heavy jacket, wool pants, and bright plaid wellies. The popular rubber boots sucked against the soggy grass with a squishing sound. "You're not going to look for clues on the beach without me, are you?"

Shannon lifted the collar of her jacket to cover her ears. "Michael asked me to call him. I thought I'd do that first."

"You'll want privacy for that."

"No. We're talking about the investigation, and that's all."

"Mm-hm," Coleen added with a knowing smirk.

"Trust me. I'm not trying to hide anything from you. I would've asked you to come with me, but I didn't think you'd want to traipse all the way up the hill with all you have to do for the show of presents tonight."

"We're pretty much ready for the guests who'll start arriving after lunch. They're staying at the castle until after the wedding, so they'll need to check in. I want to be available to welcome them, but I have free time now. Since I'm already out here, we could take a look at the beach together. Then you can go on your way alone and make your phone call."

Shannon considered it. "I suppose it doesn't matter what time I call Michael. I'm sure to wake him either way."

"Then follow me." Coleen reversed direction, nearly tripping in her oversized wellies.

"You know the way?" Shannon asked.

"Fiona told me how to get down there. She said the path is steep and guests rarely take it. She encouraged me to drive along the coast until we reach lower ground, but with all that happened to the van last night and the message painted on the side, I don't want to take it."

Shannon nodded. "It will also tell us if someone climbed the path last night."

"Didn't the police check it out?" Coleen bent her head into the wind.

Shannon followed suit. "MacGregor went up on the bluff and gave it a cursory look, but he said since I heard a car depart, it's unlikely the vandal had anything to do with the boat I 'imagined.'"

"It did seem as if he doubted it."

"And the Burkes didn't help sway him in my favor. They also believe I imagined the boat and people in the cellar."

"Not that I'm questioning you," Coleen said, pausing until Shannon looked at her, "but is it possible your imagination got carried away?"

Shannon thought about it as she approached the cliff and peered over the choppy swells of the loch. "No. I saw what I saw—lights moving on the water and across the beach. But I suppose my interpretation of what I saw might be wrong."

As a gust of wind blasted them, Coleen flipped up the hood on her coat. "What about the noises in the cellar?"

"I suppose the Burkes could be right. They know the

castle far better than I." Shannon strained her vision to see the beach, but the hazy skies kept her from locating any discernible clue. "This is the general location where I saw the lights last night, but we can't see a thing from up here. We'll have to go down to the beach to check it out."

Coleen peered over the cliff. "This is too steep. We could get hurt."

"C'mon, where's your sense of adventure?"

"I left it a few feet back, where I hadn't looked over the edge."

Shannon glanced down the path. "It's steep, but it's doable if we're careful."

Coleen didn't look convinced.

"You can stay here if you want, but I'm going down." Shannon started down the steep incline, settling her feet on wet rocks smoothed by centuries of use.

"This is worse than it looks," Coleen said from a few feet above. "I wouldn't want to run into the killer on these steps."

Shannon was thinking the same thing, but she forced it from her mind and concentrated on putting one foot in front of the other until she safely planted her feet on the firmly packed sand. Her thigh muscles screamed from the exertion, but she was proud of herself for making the trip down.

As Coleen descended, Shannon glanced around. With high tide nearly upon them, they would be restricted to a narrow swath of sand at the base of the cliff. There were no prints at the base of the steps, so if boaters had arrived last night, they hadn't climbed the cliff.

Eager to get moving, she turned and offered Coleen a hand for the last few steps. "Looks like we'll stay dry if we stick close to the cliff."

Coleen planted her feet with a solid thump. "Phew, am I glad to be down here. You might need to go behind me on the way up and push." Coleen laughed, the sound almost swallowed by the wind.

Shannon joined her friend, but her laughter quickly fell off as she scanned the area for clues. "I checked the tide table for the time I saw the boat. Would've been low tide, so any footprints except near the cliffs will have been washed away."

Coleen peered at her feet. "Let's focus on this area, then."

Keeping her head down, Shannon inched forward. About a quarter mile into their walk, she spotted two sets of prints pointing toward the cliff.

"Check out those prints," Shannon said, gesturing at the large prints made from wellies or other rain boots. "Probably from two men."

Coleen set her boot next to the smaller print. "This one is near my size."

Shannon didn't have the heart to mention Coleen's feet were large for her average height since she knew Coleen was sensitive about that, so she said, "Of course, your wellies are obviously oversized."

"Odd how they look like they both walked into the cliff."

"Maybe they did." Shannon moved closer and ran her hands over the foliage covering rough rocks. The greenery gave way under her hands, and she quickly pushed it out of the way, revealing a tunnel carved into the cliff.

"Och!" She spread the foliage farther apart so Coleen could look inside.

"We should've brought a flashlight."

"Hold this open, and I'll use the light on my cell." With

icy fingers, Shannon dug out her phone and shone it into the tunnel, which continued beyond the reach of the beam. "We'll have to go inside to see how deep it goes."

"I don't know," Coleen said hesitantly.

"Why the reluctance?" Shannon asked. "You've been hanging back at every turn, and that's so not like you." Coleen shrugged and Shannon pressed a little harder. "C'mon, it's me, remember? You can tell me anything."

"This whole wedding has me starting to feel old, like I'm on a downward slide. So I guess I've been trying to be more cautious to make sure I'm alive to see the years I have left. Silly, I know, but it's been plaguing me."

"You shouldn't let it bother you. You have many good years ahead."

"Trust me. You'll get it when one of the twins says 'I do.'" Coleen sighed. "You realize soon there will be grand-children. And if you're old enough to be a grandmother, maybe it's time to grow up, you know?"

"You, my friend, even when you're a great-great-grand-mother, will not be a grown-up in the true sense of the word—and that's what I love about you. So don't change. *Ever.*" Shannon slung an arm around Coleen and hugged her close. "Besides, I'm sure your grandkids will love the fact that you've done things like this."

Resolve claimed Coleen's face. "They will, won't they?"

"Plus, if you're old enough to be a granny, that means I'm not far behind, and I'm so not ready for that phase in my life."

"If one of your kids decides to fall in love and get married, it's not like you have any control over it."

Shannon's mouth dropped open and Coleen laughed heartily. "You can face killers, but you can't face your children growing up."

"Touché," Shannon said as she shoved the topic from her mind and focused on the tunnel. "Ready to explore?"

"Ready." Coleen lifted the foliage higher.

Shannon ducked inside the chilly, damp space. The ceiling was high enough for someone under six feet to stand comfortably. Green slime covered the walls and water leaked from above, leaving trails of sediment.

Once Coleen entered, Shannon started forward. "Stay close. This looks like it goes on for a while, and I wouldn't want to lose you."

"You don't have to tell me twice." Coleen grabbed the back of Shannon's jacket and held tight.

The tunnel made a series of turns before opening in a long, straight section.

Shannon paused to look around. "From the wear on the floor, it looks like this tunnel has been here a long time."

"I wonder if it was used to escape by boat when enemy armies invaded."

"Sounds plausible."

"I'd rather think it had to do with the whisky smuggling we read about at the distillery than think about women and children fleeing from marauding soldiers."

"I doubt anyone who owned the castle was involved in bootlegging whisky." Shannon started walking again. "This goes on much farther than I imagined. I'm going to start pacing it off as we go so I can get an idea of the depth." Shannon stepped carefully, counting as she moved. By the time they'd reached a solid door, she believed they'd traveled over one hundred feet.

Shannon turned to Coleen. "I don't have any sense of direction down here, but I'm guessing we've reached the castle."

"The sounds you heard last night could've been from someone entering the basement from the tunnel."

"My thoughts exactly."

"But why—and what were they doing?"

"I heard them dragging something heavy. Do you suppose they were loading or unloading something from the boat?" Shannon bent down and took a closer look at the floor. "No signs of anything being dragged."

"Let's try the door," Coleen suggested.

Shannon handed the light to Coleen, and she tugged on the handle. The door didn't budge, so she pushed instead. "It's locked."

"Not surprising."

Shannon took her phone from Coleen. "We need to get back to the castle and see if we can find this door in the cellar."

"After you call Michael." Coleen winked.

"Are you ever going to let this thing with Michael rest?"

"Not until this 'thing,'" she said, lifting her fingers in air quotes, "is defined and the two of you are walking down the aisle."

Shannon groaned, but as she turned away from Coleen, she smiled. Even if Coleen was pushy when it came to Shannon's love life, she loved being with her longtime friend.

After they'd both exited the tunnel, Shannon carefully re-covered it with the foliage. "Help me find something to erase our footprints so no one realizes we were here."

"That should do the trick." Coleen charged ahead and retrieved a branch lying at the edge of the surf. "You go ahead and get to the path. I'll walk in the water and erase your steps."

"Thank goodness you were sensible enough to wear your wellies."

"Tell me that again back at the castle, when I make you clean all the mud off them."

Shannon hurried back to the path and climbed onto the first stone. Coleen quickly swung the branch in arcs across the sand, then splashed water with her boots to settle and pack it back into place.

"You're a natural at that," Shannon called out.

A wide grin claimed Coleen's lips. "Comes from getting into mischief and having to cover my tracks all the time." After obliterating the last prints, she tossed the branch into the still-rising tide. "Give me your hand so I can join you without leaving prints."

Shannon tugged her friend onto the step and together they made the tortuous climb to the top. As soon as Shannon cleared the cliff, her phone rang from her pocket.

"Michael," she said to Coleen after seeing his icon appear on the screen.

"Say hello to the handsome man for me." Coleen winked. "I'll meet you back at the castle."

To hear Michael better, Shannon turned her back to the wind and greeted him with a cheerful hello.

"You didn't call," he said, sounding disappointed.

"I had to check out another lead first." As a light rain began to fall, she told him about the excitement last night and the tunnel discovery. "The vandal was a woman, which made me think it might have been Holly. I'm pretty sure the car she was driving was red."

"Want me to see if Holly Taylor owns a red car?"

"You can do that? I mean … I know you can get DMV records in America, but you've never mentioned that you have police contacts in Scotland."

"It's never come up before."

And if I don't bring it up, you don't volunteer it, she thought as she looked over the ocean with heavy clouds rolling in.

"I have a buddy in central Scotland who owes me a favor," he continued. "I could make some inquiries if you'd like."

"But would someone in that part of the country have a clue about what's going on here?"

"Scotland's eight police forces recently merged into a single Scottish service, giving my contact a connection to the inspector in your agency."

"Then I'd appreciate your help," she said. "But remember to be discreet so you don't make Watson angry."

"Now about the tunnel." Apprehension filled his words. "Please tell me you're going straight to the inspector in charge to tell him about this information."

"I have no idea if the tunnel is connected to Siobhan's murder."

"But it might be connected to what you saw last night."

"The investigating officer already dismissed the connection between the boat and the vandalism. I doubt finding a tunnel to the castle that looks like it's been there for centuries will encourage him to reconsider."

"Still, I need you to be careful," Michael warned.

"You mentioned two brides in your email." She quickly changed the subject.

"Innis Mitchell lives in Brodick and Bridget Thomson lives in Lamlash." Both towns were on the island. "They both said they ended up paying more for their weddings than they were first quoted and that they wouldn't be surprised if Siobhan scammed them."

Odd. Shannon ducked her head away from the increasing rain and considered why the brides were so forthcoming with information when it demonstrated a motive to kill Siobhan. Not coming up with a good explanation, she asked, "Why would they tell you that if one of them killed her?"

"Some people don't think before speaking and don't know their comments make them look like they have a motive for the crime," Michael said, reminding Shannon of Coleen's statements to Watson. "I also probed for an alibi, but they both clammed up when I started down that path, which automatically raised my suspicions." His cop antenna was always up and on target.

She'd do well to listen to him. "You think it's a credible lead, then?"

"Credible, maybe. They'd both read about the murder in the local paper, which means they could be stretching the truth to connect themselves to the case to get some publicity. I saw it happen often enough when I was a detective."

"Shocks me what lengths people will go to get their fifteen minutes of fame these days."

"I could be wrong about them, but without being able to see their body language, I couldn't get a good read. I thought you'd like to have a face-to-face with them."

"You're so right about that."

"Be careful, Shannon. Neither of them has a sound alibi for Siobhan's time of death, so one of them could be the killer."

Shannon surely hoped so. "If you can email me their contact information, Coleen and I have time to visit with them this afternoon."

"They promised to sit by their phones and wait for your call."

It all sounded a little too easy for Shannon, but then, Holly was the only strong suspect, so Shannon would embrace the lead with gusto. With a little luck, she'd have two additional suspects to report to the police by the end of the day.

— 16 —

Shannon couldn't eat another bite and pushed her plate away. After Melanie had snapped a group picture outside the castle, the Purls had had lunch and then departed on a caravan trip around the island with a local tour company. Shannon hated to miss the event, but time was ticking away. If she hoped to make sure Coleen was free to attend Gemma's wedding, she had to solve the mystery soon.

"I know you have your heart set on checking out the cellar, but I think we should talk to the brides first," Coleen said from across the table. "We know they're connected to Siobhan, but we have no idea if the tunnel is."

Shannon considered the change of plans. "Good point. I'm not comfortable driving through town with that message on the van, so we'll need a car. I don't suppose there's a rental agency in the village?"

"I doubt it, but we can ask Fiona." Coleen dropped her napkin on the starched white tablecloth and stood. "Let's hope she's in her office."

"Don't mention the brides," Shannon said as they made their way to the office. "Fiona was extremely fond of Siobhan, and there's no need to get her worked up if the brides' information doesn't prove embezzlement."

"We need a cover story for why we want to make the trip, but I'm not going to lie to Fiona." A fiendish look crossed Coleen's face. "I could use a bit of Shetland yarn; how about you? Feeling a need to visit Stitches?"

Shannon smiled. "I'm always willing to shop for yarn."

Cover story in place, they hurried to Fiona's office, where they found her behind her desk, her head bent over financial reports. She looked up, her face a mass of frustration. "I'm so glad you're here. Gives me an excuse to take a break before I tear my hair out." She sighed. "If only I'd studied accounting at university. I haven't a clue what I'm looking at here." She slid the papers into a folder and soundly closed it. "What can I do for you?"

Coleen stepped up to the desk. "We want to go into town, and with the message painted on its side, my van is out of commission. We hoped there was a car hire in town."

"I'm afraid not. But you could use the castle's van if it's an emergency."

"Buying Shetland wool falls under an emergency in my book. What about yours?" Coleen winked at Shannon.

Shannon laughed. "Absolutely."

"As one artist to another ..." Fiona cupped her hand around her mouth like she feared someone might hear their conversation. "I consider it an emergency and hereby grant you permission to take the van."

"Thank you." Coleen held up a hand. "I solemnly swear to drive very carefully, and we'll make a lovely scarf for you out of the wool we buy."

"That's not necessary."

"Maybe not," Shannon said, "but it gives us an excuse to buy more yarn."

Fiona's laugh tinkled behind her as she got up and

walked to a wooden box mounted on the wall. She opened the door, revealing a plethora of keys hanging on pegs. She grabbed a set with a large red key fob.

"How on earth do you keep all those keys straight?" Coleen asked.

"Greer and I know most of the castle keys by shape and size." Fiona pointed to a large silver ring filled with keys. "I suppose we should label them, but we've never found a need to do so."

Coleen took the keys from Fiona. "I'm a little too scatterbrained for that."

"Only a little," Shannon said teasingly.

"Oh, you." Coleen wrinkled her nose at Shannon, then looked at Fiona. "I won't lose these, I promise."

"That's because I'll keep an eye on them," Shannon added.

"It's lovely to see such good friends." Fiona flashed a smile, but it fell away quickly.

Shannon wondered if she was thinking about Siobhan. Shannon didn't want to sour the joyful atmosphere that had been sorely lacking with Fiona, but she had to ask about access to the financial reports. "Have you received permission for me to access the accounts?"

Fiona's lips tightened. "Sorry. The owners said that would be a breach of security and under no circumstances am I to let you into the accounts."

"I understand," Shannon said, though she didn't agree with the decision. "Thank you for trying."

"I wish I could've done more. I want to see the killer brought to justice too."

"Of course you do." Shannon squeezed Fiona's hand and bid her goodbye.

"Tough luck on the accounts," Coleen said as the friends walked down the hall.

"It was a long shot at best," Shannon said. "Let's hope the brides will provide the information we need."

"I'll work on embracing your positive attitude."

In the grand hall, Shannon said, "Let's grab our jackets and meet back here."

They split up, and Shannon made quick work of gathering her jacket and a tote that she filled with Bridget and Innis's addresses, a notepad, pen, and Coleen's wedding invoices. She unplugged her cellphone from the charger and stowed it in her pocket. Once they were in range of a cell tower, she'd phone the brides to schedule a visit.

Shannon jogged down the steps to the grand hall, where Coleen talked with Gemma. The girl's puffy eyes said she'd been crying again. Shannon didn't know if she should join them, but Gemma took the decision from her hands by rushing up to Shannon.

"Tell Mum that it's worth the price," Gemma said.

"What's worth what price?"

Coleen rubbed her shoulder through her raspberry cardigan. "Gemma wants me to pay to have calla lilies flown in for the wedding."

Gemma frowned. "But Mum won't do it."

Coleen nipped at her lower lip. "It's not that I won't, honey. We simply can't afford it."

"Sweetie." Shannon approached Gemma. "Thanks to your mum, you have an amazing dress, and you look simply breathtaking in it. Neither your groom nor your guests are going to even notice the flowers with how radiant you look."

Her frown disappeared. "I do look good, don't I?"

"The most beautiful bride I've ever seen," Shannon confirmed.

Gemma flung her arms around Shannon's neck, nearly choking her with the tight hold. Shannon extricated herself before blood ceased flowing to her head.

"You always find the perfect thing to say," Gemma said. "I wish you were my mother this week."

The pain in Coleen's expression sent an ache to Shannon's heart, and though she didn't want to meddle, she had to rectify the situation.

"Come with me." She took Gemma by the hand and led her across the room. "How can you hurt your mother this way? Do you realize all she's done to make your dream wedding come true?" she asked sternly.

Gemma shrugged.

"For starters, she's been doing without things since the day you were born to save money for your big day. She's made the most exquisite dress, and she's put up with your testy attitude all week."

"I haven't been testy," Gemma exclaimed. Shannon simply stared at the girl. "Don't look at me that way. I admit I've been a bit of a grump."

"A *bit*?"

"OK, fine." Gemma planted her hands on her hips. "A *big* grump."

"And you've taken it out on your mother, who loves you so much she'd do everything within her means to make your wedding perfect. If she could afford to fly in calla lilies, she'd do it. Don't you know that?"

Gemma looked at Coleen. "I've been a real dope."

"A simple 'thank you' and 'I love you' can make up for all of it."

Gemma crossed the space. "Mum," she said hesitantly. "I've been a real bear to live with this week. I'm so sorry. I should never have said anything like that. You're the best mum a girl could have, and I love you so much."

"Och." Tears moistened Coleen's eyes as she pulled Gemma into a hug. "I love you too, honey. So much."

Gemma pulled back. "I won't make unreasonable demands again." When Coleen arched a brow, Gemma said, "OK, fine, I might ask, but when I'm acting all self-centered, if you tell me about it, I'll stop. I promise."

Coleen grabbed Gemma's hand and shook. "We have a deal."

"Then I'm off to pick out flowers with Olivia." After casting a warm look at her mother, she slipped from the room.

"What on earth did you say to her?" Coleen asked when her daughter was out of earshot.

"The same thing you'll say to my Lara when she acts this way before her wedding."

"You can count on it."

Eager to get going, Shannon shrugged into her jacket. "Gorgeous sweater, by the way."

"Would you believe me if I said I made it?"

Shannon erupted in laughter.

"Fine. So I'm not as good as I want to be with knitting needles. I bought it at a church craft fair."

Shannon fingered the soft yarn and gauged the evenness of the stitches. "It's well made."

"You know my motto. If you can't produce quality

handiwork, at least be able to spot it for sale." Coleen grinned as they stepped into the overcast afternoon.

They found the traditional white van parked at the far end of the motor court. Coleen unlocked the doors and they both settled into the cold vinyl bucket seats. Coleen soon had them on the road, and when they climbed to the top of the first hill, Shannon dug out the brides' information. She started with Innis, quickly confirming her willingness to talk to them.

After Shannon hung up, she turned to Coleen. "Innis is home and eager to meet us. Way more eager than I would have expected."

"I'd be eager to tell you if someone ripped me off."

"Ah, but you're ready and willing to talk about anything to almost anyone."

"That I am," Coleen said. "Let's hope Bridget is too."

Shannon made the call, but had to leave a message. "Since she's not home, I guess we'll start with Innis in Brodick and we can cross our fingers that Bridget gets my message before we leave there."

They chatted about the weather and the scenery until they arrived at the first bride's home. Within a few minutes of knocking on Innis Mitchell's door, they found themselves seated on her worn sofa with a cup of tea in hand.

Innis held up a gold-rimmed cup and saucer as she settled in a club chair. "As much as I'd rather not have to talk about Siobhan's death, I seldom get to use my wedding china."

"Why do you think Siobhan embezzled from your

account?" Shannon didn't waste any time.

Innis's smile disappeared. "The costs for the wedding far exceeded our original quote."

"That's not unusual."

Innis blew on her tea and watched Shannon carefully over the rim of her cup. "It is when the wedding planner gives you an all-inclusive written quote she intends to live by but then changes her mind."

Shannon looked at Coleen. "Did you get a quote like that?"

Innis's mouth fell open. "*You* recently got married at the castle?"

"Och, no." Coleen chuckled. "My daughter is getting married on Saturday."

"And you have time to investigate Siobhan." Innis shook her head. "You're so much more together than my mother was."

"I like to think I have everything worked out," Coleen said with pride. "But we've had a few glitches."

"Namely, Siobhan's death," Shannon said, turning to Coleen. "About the quote. Did you get one too?

"Yes," Coleen said, "but she stated right up front that some items—like the flowers, for example—could change, depending on costs at the time of the wedding."

"She never told me that," Innis said, "and the contract we signed didn't mention it either."

Surprised she hadn't heard about the contract before, Shannon asked Coleen, "Did you sign a contract too?"

"Yes, but it stipulated prices were only good for thirty days. Since you book a wedding so far in advance, I looked at the contract as a document that merely confirmed my booking of the castle and Siobhan's services."

"She probably had so many complaints about price gouging that she had to change the contract," Innis said.

"How did she handle your complaint?"

"She got defensive and never gave me a very satisfactory explanation. I wanted to explore it further, but honestly, I was so stressed about paying the bills, and with the wedding around the corner, I didn't have the strength." She sighed. "Now I wish I had. You'd be sitting on a nice leather sofa right now instead of that ratty old thing if the money hadn't gone for the wedding."

But was the loss of the money enough of a reason to commit murder? "If you still have the invoices and contract from the wedding, I'd like to look at them if you don't mind."

"Of course." Innis set down her cup and stood. "Let me get them."

When she'd left the room, Shannon turned to Coleen. "While I review the information, will you probe for an alibi for Siobhan's time of death?"

"I'm the queen of chitchat. Let me work my magic on her."

"OK, but do it subtly," Shannon said, wondering if Coleen knew the meaning of the word.

Innis returned with a large divided folder. She pulled out a stack of papers and handed them to Shannon.

"Would you mind if I took the time to compare these to Coleen's invoices?"

"Not at all." Innis grabbed her cup again. "It's good to

have time to sit and savor a cup of tea for a change."

Shannon pulled Coleen's invoices from her bag and spread out all the pages as she kept her ears tuned for a chance to place well-timed questions.

"How's married life treating you?" Coleen asked.

"Fine," Innis said unenthusiastically, bringing Shannon's head up in time to catch a flash of sadness on Innis's face. Was there trouble in her marriage this soon?

"I remember the early days, don't you Shannon?" Coleen asked. "Learning to live with someone can be hard."

Shannon nodded. "As is finding out the man of your dreams has flaws like every human being."

"Sometimes major ones." Innis's lower lip quivered.

Coleen sat forward. "You sound so sad. Would you like to talk about it?"

Innis shrugged as her eyes filled with tears.

"You poor thing," Coleen said, and Shannon knew Coleen was no longer fishing for information but wanted to help the young woman. "We're both mothers, and I'd like to think we can help. Go ahead and tell us what the big oaf has done to make you so upset."

"Rory's cheating on me." Tears slipped free and rolled over high cheekbones. "We haven't even been married for six months, and he's cheating."

Coleen grabbed a tissue from her bag and handed it to Innis. "Are you sure?"

"Positive." Innis dabbed her eyes. "We couldn't afford to book the castle exclusively, so we shared our wedding day with another couple. The Thomsons. Bridget and Aiden." Innis sobbed, and Coleen patted her knee.

Shannon perked up more. The bride they were going to visit next was named Bridget Thomson, and the urge to blurt out questions was nearly too strong for Shannon to bear. She bit her lip to keep from speaking when Innis was so upset, and she let Coleen continue to take lead.

"Now what does this other couple have to do with your Rory?" Coleen asked sympathetically.

"We stayed at the castle the week before the wedding, as did the Thomsons. We liked each other and bonded. It's so hard to find another couple that you both like and who live close by. So when I saw Rory and Bridget getting along so well, I was thrilled." Innis looked up and sniffled. "But then it seemed as if they were getting too chummy."

"What did you do?"

"I confronted Rory, that's what. He said they simply had a lot in common. They both work for CalMac Ferries and could swap crazy stories about passengers. He was so convincing that I felt guilty for asking and dropped it, but now…" She paused to blow her nose. "Now I know better."

"What makes you think he's cheating?" Coleen asked gently.

"A few weeks ago, he started going to work earlier. Said he was up for a promotion and wanted to show them he was fit for the job. On Thursday night when we were out with the Thomsons, Aiden said they couldn't stay out late because Bridget had changed ferries, and she had to go to work earlier. I thought it odd that they both started going to work early and alarm bells went off in my head. So I

188 S U S A N   S L E E M A N

followed Rory the next morning. Caught him meeting
Bridget at a local restaurant for breakfast."

"Oh my," Coleen said. "What did you do?"

"I called Aiden, and we both followed them on
Monday morning. They were going to check into a
motel. Rory claims they hadn't done it before, but it didn't
matter to me. I can't be with someone who even thinks
about cheating."

"I'm so sorry, Innis," Coleen said.

Unable to keep quiet any longer, Shannon asked, "What
time did you and Aiden catch them?"

"Not that it matters, but it was around five o'clock."

"What did you do after you found them?" Shannon
asked.

"Hah! You're not going to believe this." Her face suddenly burned with anger. "We all went to the Thomsons'
house to have a civilized conversation. Not that it worked.
We yelled at each other for an hour, then Rory and I came
home, and I hollered at him all morning before kicking
him out."

Shannon met Coleen's gaze, confirming that Coleen
had inadvertently stumbled upon both Innis and Bridget's
alibis.

"You must be reeling from this," Coleen said.

Innis sneered. "Now you know why I want to see
Siobhan's embezzlement come out. Maybe I can get some
of my money back to use it in the divorce." She tipped her
head at the invoices. "Will those help?"

"Not likely." Shannon gathered the pages together. "But
if you'll let me take them, they might help me solve this

case. If we find out you're due any money, we'll make sure you receive it."

"You're welcome to the file and to make copies if you want as long as I get the information back." Innis pulled back her shoulders and stood. "I'm sorry for blubbering all over you, but I appreciate your support."

After Shannon gathered up the papers, Innis showed them to the door. As soon as she closed it Coleen said, "Poor thing, having to go through that. But it *does* give her an alibi."

"That it does, along with Bridget as well." Shannon said. "And that leaves us with Holly as our only suspect."

They climbed into the van, and Shannon saw a red car speed past, which gave her an idea. "Since we don't have to go see Bridget, let's go ahead and drive over to Holly's place. If she's back home, maybe we can find out if she has a red car."

"And if not, we can ask her neighbor," Coleen said, catching Shannon's enthusiasm. "I'll have us there in a jiffy."

Shannon used the travel time to think about what they would do next. She pulled out her notepad and tapped her pen against her chin as she watched the miles of coastline fly by. Where should she start?

Since she'd ruled out all the suspects except Holly and they hadn't learned anything new about her, Shannon needed to locate someone else who had a reason to want to end Siobhan's life. But who?

She tapped a little harder. Maybe another staff member at the castle.

She made a note to interview the castle staff again.

Maybe she should even look into Fiona and Greer. Though she knew of no motive for them to kill Siobhan, she hadn't considered them before. She added "Research Fiona and Greer" to her list.

As they pulled up in front of Holly's house and Shannon didn't see a car in the driveway, she jotted "Call Michael about Holly's car" on the pad too. Even if they discovered Holly drove a red car, Shannon wanted official proof to encourage Watson to investigate Holly.

"Looks like we'll be talking to the neighbor again." Shannon stowed her stuff.

"That should be interesting." Coleen turned off the engine.

They climbed out and headed straight for the neighbor's front door where Coleen pounded loud enough to wake the dead. The woman answered so fast Shannon guessed she had been watching out the window.

She leaned against the doorjamb. "Well, you're back for more, are ya?"

"Does Holly own a car, and if so, what type and color?" Coleen blurted out.

The woman snorted. "So much for the pleasantries."

"Sorry about that," Shannon said. "We don't mean to be rude, but we're in a bit of a hurry."

"Och, aren't we all, these days?"

Shannon didn't want to engage her in small talk, so she simply waited for her to speak. "She has a small import. Don't know the brand, but it's red as a barn so everyone can see her coming."

Shannon wanted to jump up and down for joy at their discovery—until she realized that Holly, the most

obsessed person Shannon had ever investigated, had left
a warning message last night, and, if Shannon didn't
give up the investigation, Holly could be planning to end
Shannon's life.

— 17 —

Thursday evening, Shannon stood before the Purls and Coleen. They'd all changed into dressier attire for the show of presents and were seated on the settee and chairs in front of the roaring fireplace in Shannon's lavish bedroom.

"We need your help, ladies," Shannon announced. "This morning we discovered a secret tunnel running from the cliff to the castle cellar. We don't know if it was used to access the castle when Siobhan was killed, but we suspect as much."

"A secret tunnel. How exciting." Betty clapped her hands. Her vivid aqua sweater moved in rhythm and reminded Shannon of an ocean wave. "How can we help?"

"The door to the cellar was locked," Shannon answered. "If we can get down to the cellar without being seen, we hope to find where it leads. That's where you all come in."

Melanie feigned an evil grin, then twisted an imaginary handlebar moustache. "Just the sound of it makes me want to help you do whatever you need. I'm in for sure."

"How can you agree when Shannon hasn't even said what we have to do?" Betty asked.

"I don't care what it is," Melanie said enthusiastically. "I'm a sucker for secret tunnels, so count me in."

"Thanks." Shannon squeezed Melanie's shoulder. "For the rest of you, we need someone to distract Fiona and

Greer and someone to stand guard at the kitchen door."

"What about the kitchen staff?" Betty asked.

"They take a fifteen-minute break very soon," Coleen said. "And I've already invited them, along with Fiona and Greer, to the banquet room to sample the catered refreshments we'll serve at the show of presents."

Betty arched a brow. "I'm surprised you catered the food when there's a kitchen staff on site."

"Trust me, it wasn't my idea," Coleen said. "Gemma read about this five-star caterer in a bridal magazine, and she wanted to hire them for the entire reception. I couldn't possibly afford that, so we settled on catering the show of presents and letting the castle staff do the reception."

"Oh, it's a *bride* thing." Betty laughed. "Are you sure fifteen minutes is enough time to get down to the cellar and back?"

"It should be if everyone can help," Shannon replied.

"I'll take on Greer," Betty offered. "We can chat about the hospitality business."

"I'm a natural for Fiona." Joyce waved her fingers, clad in sparkly rings, in the air. "She's the only person I've ever met who likes bling as much as I do."

"I never thought I'd live to see the day you could say that." Betty laughed and the Purls joined in until Coleen clapped her hands, stilling them.

"With your hostess skills, Mel," Shannon continued, "you'd do an excellent job of keeping the kitchen staff occupied in the banquet room."

"Aw, I hoped I'd get to go down to the cellar with you." She tugged the lapels of her green blazer tight and sat up straighter. "But if you need me with the staff, I'm your girl."

"I guess I can stand guard," Kate offered reluctantly. "Though I'm not sure how my skills qualify me for the job."

"Are you kidding?" Coleen stood, her bright red party dress swirling into place. "Anyone who can keep track of more than one dog at a time the way you do can surely spot someone coming."

"OK, I'll do it," Kate said more enthusiastically.

"Great." Coleen tapped her jeweled watch. "Now to synchronize our watches."

"Really?" Excitement colored Kate's voice.

"She's pulling your leg," Shannon said, and Kate's smile fell. "But do remember to check the clock once the staff arrives in the banquet room. That way you'll know when our fifteen minutes is nearing its end. If Coleen and I haven't returned in time, you'll need to stall."

Everyone checked their watches and gathered their bags and shawls before they stood, ready to go.

"OK." Shannon's heart fluttered with excitement, and she took a deep breath. "Let's get downstairs and greet the staff."

The women filed out, but Kate lingered. "You can count on me, you know. After everything you did to help clear my name in Millicent's death, I have your back for life."

"And I yours." Shannon hugged the young woman, whom she thought of as a little sister.

They all hurried down the stairs to a small banquet room used for intimate gatherings. The space boasted the same red flocked wallpaper, heavy brocade drapes, and antique furniture as the library and drawing room. But the middle of

the space held round tables draped with linen cloths under
a massive crystal chandelier.

Joyce's face lit up the moment she spotted the long buffet table along the wall. It was covered with rich pastries
and a colorful punch provided by the caterers. "Do I have
time to sample? For professional reasons, of course."

"Purely professional, I'm sure." Coleen laughed. "But
yes, everyone help yourselves to the goodies. We've ordered
plenty, and the trays will be replenished before the show of
presents begins."

"I can't wait to see your traditions in action." Joyce
grabbed a finger sandwich. "It will be interesting to compare the event with our bridal showers back home."

As they waited for the staff, Shannon felt jittery. So
when a knock sounded on the door, she jumped.

Cook Rhona poked her head around the corner. "Are
you ready for us?"

"Come in," Coleen cried out as she bustled across the
room. "Help yourself to the refreshments."

Leading the staff members into the room, Rhona eyed
the buffet longingly. "What a lovely table. It's a joy to be the
one sampling the goodies instead of making them."

Shannon stood back and watched everyone file in and
fill their plates with pastries and appetizers. When Fiona
and Greer joined the crowd, Shannon tugged on Coleen's
arm and made her way to the exit. Kate joined them at the
door and the trio set off.

"I feel like I'm back in my rebellious teen years, afraid
that a grown-up will catch me," Kate said breathlessly.

Coleen glanced behind them. "We'll have a hard time

explaining our actions if we get caught."

"We won't get caught." Shannon stopped at the kitchen door. "Stand guard here, Kate. Hurry to the steps and call down to us if you hear anyone coming."

"Will you be able to get back upstairs in time?"

"We'll worry about that if it happens." Shannon took Coleen's arm. "We need to get going."

They zoomed through the warm kitchen, which smelled of pungent herbs, to the cellar door. Shannon pulled on the knob and was surprised when it didn't budge. "It's locked."

"That *proves* they're hiding something." Resolve claimed Coleen's expression. "I'm sure of it."

"Or it's not safe for people to go down there, so they've locked it to protect the guests."

"Hah. How many guests would want to go in the cellar?"

"Besides us, you mean."

"Exactly."

Shannon considered it. "I suppose with the many secret passages, guests might be more prone to explore in hopes of finding some age-old secret."

"True." Coleen looked around the room. "But how do we find a key?"

"From what we saw in Fiona's office, I'm sure she must have one."

"Did you see all the keys in her cabinet?" Coleen's brow furrowed. "How will we find the right key in the time we have?"

"We'll need a distraction that will keep her out of the way until I figure out which key it is."

"We can't lure the staff out of here again. We'll have to

come back later tonight, after the party and after the staff has gone home."

"Agreed." Shannon couldn't still the apprehension she felt. She was all for finding out what lay behind the heavy door, but after the strange noises she'd heard coming from the cellar and the incident last night, she didn't relish the idea of visiting the cellar in the dark of night.

* * *

Friday morning broke dreary and cold. Shannon's dread had proved groundless. Fiona had locked her office before retiring for the night, keeping Shannon and Coleen from securing a cellar key. Another night lost without locating a new, strong lead, so they would have to make good use of their time today if they were going to clear Coleen's name before the wedding.

Shannon slid closer to Coleen to make sure the waitstaff wouldn't overhear them as they cleared the table. "I need you to get Fiona out of the office so I can nab the keys. You could ask to see her painting again. She was eager to show you her work before, and she'd likely cooperate again."

"That should work, but I'm not sure how long I can keep her occupied, so you'll have to work fast." Coleen sipped her tea. "What have you decided to do about the kitchen staff? You can't waltz past them to the cellar door without an explanation."

"Rhona seems reasonable. I'll simply tell her what I'm doing. Minus admitting I swiped the keys, of course."

"Do you really think this will work?"

"With the wedding tomorrow, do we have any other choice?"

"No."

"We should get going, then." Shannon rose and marched toward Fiona's office. Outside a powder room a few doors away, she stopped and whispered, "I'll wait in here. Be sure you talk loudly when you pass by so I know you're leaving."

"I think I can handle that part." Coleen grinned.

"Trust me, I know all too well that you can, but be sure not to be so loud that it makes her suspicious." Shannon ducked into the small room with an antique dresser serving as a vanity and an old-fashioned pull-chain toilet. She pressed her ear to the door, but she needn't have bothered. As Coleen approached, her voice echoed from the stone walls. When her voice faded to nothing, Shannon poked her head out, then ran down to the office, where she found the door unlocked and the large ring of keys, as expected.

She slipped it into her sweater pocket, and as she turned to leave, her sweater caught on a pile of newspapers, sending them to the floor. She gathered them up, but when she spotted the Glasgow newspaper open to the Arts and Entertainment page, she paused. Big, bold headlines announced, "Corot Painting Stolen from Local Gallery."

Shannon scanned the details and was stunned to see that the stolen painting was titled *Landscape at Coubron* by Corot. The very painting Coleen had heard Fiona talking about.

Coincidence? Not likely. But what did it mean, and could it be related to Siobhan's death? Shannon would check it out after she investigated the cellar.

She was hurrying down the hallway toward the kitchen

when a loud commotion in the grand hall caught her attention. Inspector Watson's booming voice mixed with Coleen's in an explosive argument. Shannon caught only bits and pieces, but what she heard didn't sit well with her.

She rushed to the room to intercede and found Watson standing alongside Constables MacGregor and Brodie, facing Coleen. She'd planted her hands on her hips, and anger darkened her face. Looking mortified, the genteel Fiona stood next to Coleen. Fire blazed from Watson's eyes. Coleen had obviously angered him, but why? She'd only make things worse.

"I'll not be having my private space invaded at your whim," Coleen snarled.

"It's not my whim, Mrs. Douglas." Watson held out an official-looking document. "If you'd be reasonable and take a look at the mandate to search your room, you'll see I'm within my rights."

"*I'll* look at it," Shannon offered.

Coleen spun, her expression a mix of worry and gratitude at seeing Shannon. "Thank goodness you're here."

Shannon moved toward her friend, careful not to jostle her pocket and make the castle keys jingle.

Watson flashed a relieved look at Shannon. "If Mrs. Douglas agrees, I'll be glad to show the paperwork to you."

"Go ahead, then," Coleen said as she eased closer to Shannon.

Shannon took the paperwork and turned away from Watson. She made great pretense of scanning the document, though she had no idea what she should be looking for.

"Did you get the you-know-whats from the office?" Coleen whispered.

"In my pocket," Shannon whispered back. "If you can handle Watson on your own, this might be the perfect way to keep Fiona busy for a while."

"No way. He's planning to search my room. I need you there in case I run into more trouble."

Shannon felt the keys burning a hole in her pocket, but she wouldn't leave Coleen alone with Watson. "I'll put the keys back for now. Then we'll try this again when Watson leaves."

"OK."

Shannon returned the document to Watson. "I'm assuming you won't mind if I accompany all of you to Coleen's room?"

Watson sighed. "You may join us."

"I need to make a quick stop in the powder room, and then I'm all yours." Shannon hurried away before Watson could object. She heard Fiona try to excuse herself, but Coleen asked her to stay until Shannon returned.

She made quick work of returning the keys and then rejoined the group.

Watson peered at Coleen. "Would you please lead the way?"

They tromped to Coleen's suite, and after donning latex gloves, the officers began a systematic search of the space. They started in the sitting room, flipping over sofa and chair cushions and digging in the seats, but they failed to produce any evidence.

"I told you that you had nothing to worry about," Shannon said to Coleen as they followed the men into the bedroom.

Coleen eyed Watson skeptically. "They're not done yet."

"Let's split up," Watson announced. "MacGregor, you take the bathroom. Brodie, the bedroom. I'll do the wardrobe."

Shannon positioned herself near the bathroom doorway so she could see both rooms.

Watson fumbled around in the drawer and pulled out Coleen's jewelry box. He flipped open the top and stared inside. "Well, well, well—what do we have here?"

"If you're thinking I killed Siobhan for money to buy my jewelry, it's not real, you know. Just costume junk."

Watson set the leather box on the nightstand. "It's not the jewelry that I find interesting."

Shannon cast a questioning look at Coleen.

Coleen shrugged. "There's nothing in there but my jewelry."

Watson made a show of pulling an evidence bag from his jacket pocket and shaking it out before he reached inside the jewelry box and took out a slivery object that flashed in the overhead light.

Coleen gasped and grabbed Shannon's arm.

"What is it?" Shannon asked, her focus fixed on Watson.

Without a word, he held the wine bottle stopper up, giving Shannon a clear view.

"The murder weapon," Shannon whispered disbelievingly as her heart sank. She'd failed to find the real killer—and it looked like Watson would arrest Coleen the day before her daughter's wedding.

— 18 —

"**I** didn't put it there!" Coleen exclaimed.

Watson fixed a practiced interrogator's glare on Coleen. "Then who did?"

Coleen crossed her arms. "I don't know, but it wasn't me."

Recovering from the shock, Shannon cleared her head and asked Coleen, "When was the last time you looked in the jewelry case?"

"Last night. To get out a pair of earrings to wear to the show of presents." She pointed at her nightstand. "I was too tired to put them away, and I didn't bother with jewelry this morning."

"So whoever put the stopper in there had to have done so after six last night."

"They probably did it while we were all busy at the event."

"Or you put it there yourself," Watson said.

Shannon ignored his comment and considered who would have access to Coleen's room. Maids, caretakers, Gemma, and Olivia. Fiona and Greer. Maybe even Holly. She'd worked at the castle, after all.

"Holly Taylor," Shannon said aloud before thinking it through. "She could have had a master key made for the rooms before she was fired, then snuck in here to hide the bottle stopper and pin the murder on Coleen. *If* she'd located a locksmith to duplicate the key without asking too many questions."

Watson shook his head. "Solid thinking, but Holly's been in custody since early yesterday afternoon."

"What?" Coleen asked. "You didn't mention that."

"That was on my list to cover with you after the search." He pulled out his small notebook and flipped the pages. "She was apprehended as she boarded the afternoon ferry. She admitted to spray-painting your van. She was angry that the two of you were asking questions about her and making the locals think she'd killed Siobhan. It became clear in our interrogation that she is suffering from mental illness, and she's been hospitalized for a psychiatric evaluation."

"She could have broken out of the hospital."

"*Now* who's suffering from delusions?" Watson asked, digging out his phone. "I will humor you and call the hospital now to confirm her presence."

He stepped away from them while his men continued searching.

Worried that Holly was now ruled out and they had no other suspects, Shannon pulled Coleen to the corner of the room. "Do you think it could be the Burkes?"

"The Burkes? No. I can't see it. They're such a sweet couple. A little odd, but sweet."

"I thought the same thing, but I saw a Glasgow paper in their office with a story about a painting stolen from a Glasgow gallery. It's the painting you heard her talking about with Greer."

"So?"

"What if she paints the pictures so they can steal the originals and replace them with copies so no one knows they're gone? Maybe Siobhan caught on to them, and they killed her."

Coleen snorted. "Art thieves. Really, Shannon. I want to believe it, but that's even more farfetched than thinking they're killers."

"I suppose I could be grasping at straws, but we've run out of other options." Shannon thought about the couple and remembered how they'd been nearby on both nights she'd heard noises in the basement. "I need to get down to the cellar. If they're involved in art theft, I'll bet I'll find proof down there. Can I go now?"

"What if Watson arrests me?"

"I'm afraid he will if I don't find a viable alternative."

"But Gemma's wedding ... I can't miss my sweet baby's wedding."

"I won't let that happen."

"Go. Now. Before I change my mind."

Shannon hugged her friend, then ran out of the room. She could only hope and pray Fiona wasn't in her office. If she was, Shannon didn't have a clue as to how she would get hold of the keys.

* * *

Shannon needn't have worried. Fiona was nowhere in sight, and Shannon quickly nabbed the keys and then ran upstairs to her room for a jacket. She planned to try the keys on the tunnel side of the door, as she couldn't risk the kitchen staff stopping her when Watson was so close to arresting Coleen.

With a countdown clock to Coleen's arrest ticking in Shannon's head, she moved as fast as she could to the cliff, then started down the steep rock steps. Rain pelted her back and her smooth-soled shoes slid on the wet stones. She should've thought to change shoes, but the idea hadn't occurred to her. She grabbed tall foliage wherever possible, and after a few harrowing minutes, she made it to the beach. Her shoes sank into the sand, and water instantly flooded inside, sucking the shoes from her feet. The chill had her drawing in her breath, but she ignored the cold, and after pulling her shoes from the muck, she hurried to the opening on bare feet.

Using her phone for light, she slipped into the tunnel and sighed for joy over the lack of rain. Her jacket was soaked through. She swiped wet hair from her face and bent to put on her gritty shoes. Despite her discomfort, she rushed through the tunnel. Her heels clicked a steady beat on the stone. She'd rather not let anyone know she was coming, but her feet were already icy cold, and they would soon be numb if she took off her shoes.

She rounded the corner and reached the door. It was still locked, so she tucked her phone under her chin and pulled out the keys. One by one, she sifted them through fingers stiff from the cold until the ancient tumblers clicked open.

"Yes!" she whispered as she pushed the heavy door open. It groaned with age, the rusty hinges grating on her nerves. Instead of finding the cellar as she'd thought, another tunnel led away from her. A hint of warmth filtered through the space, however, giving her hope that she'd moved into the castle.

She slipped out of her shoes to keep from making any

noise, the stone floor a chilly shock to her system. She shivered violently and shone her light ahead as she moved silently over the floor. She spotted several sets of large footprints on the dusty stone—footprints similar to the ones she and Coleen had seen outside the tunnel yesterday.

A corner loomed ahead. Holding her breath, she swung around it and shone her light ahead. The cellar she'd expected opened in front of her. A large space, it had a low ceiling. Thick cobwebs hung from the rafters except directly above the walkway, making her think someone took the route often. A monster of a furnace with pipes clanking and groaning as they fed the massive boiler sat ahead of her.

The pipes could have made the dragging sounds she'd heard, and the hissing of the boiler could sound like voices through the floor. Had she been wrong about the noises? If she was, Coleen was going to miss her daughter's wedding.

Redoubling her resolve, Shannon moved forward, inching past the furnace.

A hand suddenly shot out from the dark and clamped over her mouth and jerked her back against what she thought was a tall man's body. He immediately pressed the cold steel of a knife against her throat.

She screamed, but it came out muffled from behind the thick fingers. He knocked her cell from her hand, dousing the light. The space sank into darkness, save the indirect light from the fire under the furnace.

With a knife to her throat, she knew not to fight her captor, so she stood still while waiting for directions. He remained silent. Why wasn't he saying or doing anything? Did he plan to kill her right here, or was he waiting for someone else?

"What do you want with me?" she asked, her voice muffled and trembling.

He didn't answer.

She waited, shivering in the cold, her feet stiffening and feeling like they were freezing to the floor. Her mind raced for ways to escape before her captor harmed her.

Finally, a gas lantern moved at the far side of the cellar, swinging back and forth as someone carried it forward. She couldn't make out who it was, but before long, the person set it on the ground and retreated into the shadows. She heard a sound like a large stone rolling across the floor. The very sound she'd heard last night. Then a key turning a lock and a door swinging open on rusty hinges.

She heard the footsteps of the other person recede, and the man nudged her forward. The lantern cast sufficient light to keep her from stumbling, but not enough light to fully reveal her surroundings.

When they reached the lantern, the man turned and eased her toward an open door. At the threshold, he snatched the keys from her hand, shoved her inside, and slammed the door. Without the lantern light, the darkness was stifling.

The massive stone grated across the floor outside, and Shannon's heart tightened like a fist. They'd sealed her in this room, and she couldn't help but think her abductors had left her here to die.

— 19 —

In Apple Grove, Michael Stone leaned back in his desk chair at Stone & McCrary and stretched his arms overhead. He'd stayed up late the last few nights, looking into the brides and the car registration for Holly, and his work was suffering.

His phone rang, and the caller ID announced Nils Ventura, owner of Ventura Gallery in Portland. One of Michael's important clients, Nils called only when he had a problem. Michael quickly grabbed the phone.

"Nils," Michael answered and stifled a yawn. "What can I do for you today?"

"That recent art theft has me spooked, and I wanted to schedule time with you to review our security plan. You can never be too careful when it comes to security."

Michael subscribed to news aggregate services to keep up-to-date on areas relating to his client's businesses, but he'd arrived late and hadn't read the news. Not something he wanted to tell an important client.

"How recent are we talking about?" he asked, hoping to draw the news out of Nils.

"Yesterday. Someone stole a Jean-Baptiste-Camille Corot painting from a Scotland gallery. They're not sure how long it's been missing. The thief replaced it with an exquisite copy. An observant worker caught the switch when she noticed a nick in the frame."

An exquisite copy, perhaps from a caretaker at the very castle where Shannon was staying?

Michael dropped his feet to the floor and sat at attention. "Say the painter's name again."

"Jean-Baptiste-Camille Corot."

"And the name of the painting?" Michael held his breath as he waited for the answer.

"*Landscape at Coubron.* Do you know something about it?"

"No," Michael said, his heart sinking. "But someone mentioned it to me this week, and I'd like to follow up with them."

"The authorities believe this heist was pulled off by the same person who's lifted a number of paintings in Scotland."

Michael had to get off the phone and call Shannon. "When would you like to get together?"

"Is tomorrow too soon?"

Depends if Shannon's found herself in the middle of a murder and an art heist.

"The afternoon works for me," he said, hoping the issue with Shannon would be resolved by then. "I can come by your gallery around two."

"Perfect," Nils replied. "Thanks for humoring me. I'll see you then."

Michael disconnected and immediately pressed Shannon's icon on his phone. He got up and paced as the phone rang. Once. Twice. Three times; then to voice mail. He left a quick message and then logged on to his computer. He found the phone number for Hamilton Castle and dialed. Many rings later, an answering machine clicked on.

Not good. Someone on staff should answer during business hours. But if the job fell to the caretakers and they were art thieves, he doubted they much cared about a good work ethic. In case he was mistaken about their actions, he left an urgent message to have Shannon call him.

He could phone each of the Purls and Coleen, but first he needed their phone numbers. He grabbed a local phone book and ran his finger down the A's, then dialed Tom Russo at the inn.

"Apple Grove Inn," Tom answered cheerfully.

"Tom, it's Michael Stone. I need to get ahold of Shannon, and with the iffy cell reception there, she's not answering. I wondered if you could give me Joyce's number so I can try her."

"Did you try calling the castle number?" Tom asked.

"Yes, but there was no answer."

"Not a good way to run a business."

"Agreed." Michael's concern for Shannon was growing, and he was losing patience. "Would you mind giving me Joyce's number?"

"No problem." Tom rattled off the number.

"Do you have any of the other Purls' cell numbers?"

"If you hold on, I can go to the office and look in Joyce's contact file."

"Thanks," Michael replied as visions of Shannon under the control of a notorious art thief kept his foot tapping on the floor. He got up and paced until Tom came back on the phone.

"Got them all," Tom said.

Michael grabbed a notepad and jotted the numbers down. "I don't suppose Coleen Douglas's number is there."

"No, sorry."

"Thanks, Tom. If Joyce happens to call again, would you tell her I'm urgently trying to get in touch with Shannon?"

"Say, is there something wrong? Something I need to know about?"

"No. I'm just helping Shannon with something," Michael said, coming as close to a lie as he was willing to get. "Thanks again, Tom." He disconnected before Tom could ask for details.

He dialed Joyce. No answer. In turn, he tried Betty, Melanie, and Kate, all with no luck. Then he sat back to formulate a plan. Perhaps his contact at the Police Service of Scotland could tell him if they had any leads on the theft and if those leads were tied to Hamilton Castle. He quickly computed the time difference and hoped Gavin wouldn't have gone home for the day. If he had and Shannon was in trouble, Michael didn't know what to do next.

*   *   *

Shannon felt around the walls until she found a light switch and flipped it. When her eyes adjusted, she looked around the space, which was about ten feet by ten feet in size. The walls and ceiling were drywall with modern air vents dispersed around the room. An electronic thermostat hung on the wall, and the room was significantly warmer than the rest of the cellar. Clearly, the room was a later addition to the castle.

She wasn't surprised to see three paintings on the far wall, one of which she recognized from the newspaper photo of *Landscape at Coubron*. Probably not the one Fiona painted, but the original stolen from the museum. Additionally, several large sculptures sat on pedestals dispersed around the room.

"Paintings and sculptures," she mumbled. "The Burkes' specialties."

Still, the Burkes' side business had nothing to do with Siobhan. As Shannon studied the paintings, voices filtered through the vents, drawing her attention. She eased closer to a vent.

"We can't leave her there. That's cruel." Shannon recognized the voice as Fiona's.

"Besides, we have to get the paintings out," she heard a man say.

"Greer," Fiona chastised, "I'm beginning to wonder if killing Siobhan has dulled your compassion."

Shannon gasped at Fiona's admission.

"I'm sorry, dear, but if we don't fence the paintings, then Siobhan's death will have been in vain."

"But," Fiona said, "if we leave now, we'll evade the murder charge. No one can prove you killed Siobhan. With the murder weapon stashed in Coleen's room, she'll take the fall."

"And now *you're* the one saying we should leave Mrs. McClain in there."

"Yes. Just for a bit, until we're long gone. Then we send an anonymous tip to locate her."

"She'll simply rat us out."

"How can she? We were careful to make sure she didn't see us just now."

"The Corot painting will tie us to the room," Greer said sharply.

"Loosely, maybe, but there's no proof that we put her in there."

"Our prints are all over the room."

"Assuming they ever find us, which I doubt, they'll get us for theft. That's a far cry from murder."

"We're the only ones who know the room exists, so how could anyone else have put her in there?"

"We'll set up another staff member before we take off, just like we framed Siobhan for embezzlement and Coleen for her murder."

"Look how well both of those attempts worked." Sarcasm filled Greer's voice. "You should've let me kill Siobhan the minute she caught us coming back from that heist instead of trying your complicated scheme. Framing her for embezzlement to get her arrested before she found our cellar room took way too long and was too risky. I *knew* one of the brides would spot the changes in their invoices."

Shannon's mouth dropped open. Poor Siobhan. They'd set her up. She wasn't even guilty of a crime.

"It's not my fault the plan didn't work. I could've handled the bride. It's all nosy Coleen's fault. If she hadn't overheard us and confronted Siobhan like that, Siobhan wouldn't have known a thing about our tampering with the books until the police arrived to arrest her."

"I suppose," Greer said reluctantly.

"A frame-up is the perfect solution now," Fiona said with enthusiasm. "Trust me. With the short time we have to make this happen, the chance of anyone discovering it is miniscule."

"And what if, with all the police roaming around the place, we can't manage that?"

A long moment of silence filled the space. "Then you have your way, my love," Fiona said. "Shannon McClain dies."

*　*　*

As Michael answered his ringing cell, visions of the many times Shannon had found herself in trouble flashed into his brain. He'd always been nearby, but now she was half the world away, and he couldn't help her. His mind flashed back to his days as a Portland police detective. He'd also been powerless to help Angela. If he couldn't help his own wife in the same town, how could he expect to help someone halfway around the world?

The call was from Gavin, and as he answered the phone, Michael prepared himself to hear that Shannon had been hurt. Or was missing. Or … no, he wouldn't go there.

"Stone," Michael barked into the phone.

"Good to hear from you, mate," Gavin said pleasantly.

"Is Shannon OK?"

"Now who would this Shannon be?" Gavin asked.

"You're not calling to tell me she's hurt?'

"No, I'm phoning you about the stolen Corot you were asking about. You didn't mention a Shannon, though she sounds mighty important to you. Maybe you should have."

Michael exhaled. "What do you know about the Corot?"

"Nothing much, I'm afraid—other than it was replaced by a remarkable forgery."

"I'm pretty sure you can find your forger at Hamilton Castle." Michael recounted the details of his conversations with Shannon. "I've been unable to find any records for a Fiona and Greer Burke, so that's probably not their real names. The castle website doesn't have any photos of them, so I can't even help you there."

"Any chance Shannon could snap a pic and send it to us?"

Michael paced. "She's not answering her phone. Neither are any of her friends, nor is anyone at the castle. I'm beginning to think the worst."

"Explains your earlier attitude."

"I don't suppose you could arrange to have an officer stop by the castle?"

"Of course. I'll call them right now, but the Arran office has a small staff, so without evidence of a real crime, it might take a bit of time to dispatch them. *If* they even agree to make the trek out to the castle."

"Tell them they're helping solve an art theft. That should get any small-town cop moving."

Gavin chuckled. "Right you are."

"Will you call me the minute you hear back from them?"

"Of course, but I'm headed into a mandatory debriefing on a murder, so it may take a few hours before I can follow up with the officers in Hamilton. I'd bow out, but it's a grisly case, and we need to do everything we can to find this bugger."

"I appreciate anything you can do, Gavin."

"Let me give you my cell number. That way you can reach me directly in the event one of your friends at the castle calls with information I can pass on."

Michael jotted the number on his notepad. As soon

as he hung up, he saved the number in his phone's address book. Michael didn't want to think about being half a world away and getting a call that Shannon was in danger. But if that call ever came, he wanted to be prepared.

It could mean the difference between life and death.

— 20 —

Shannon had to formulate an escape plan. But what? Even if she could find something to use to pick the lock, it had sounded like the Burkes had rolled a stone in place outside the door. Her only hope was to find something to use as a weapon to defend herself against them if they decided to retrieve the paintings.

She wandered the room in search of something serviceable. She lifted the Corot painting down from the wall and eyed the wire strung across the back. The heavy-gauge wire would work fine to strangle someone. *If* she were able to disable someone that way, which she highly doubted.

She moved on to the other paintings and found the same wire and fasteners. She could tear out the painting and use the wood frame to protect herself, but she didn't feel good about destroying a priceless piece of art before exploring every option.

In the middle of the room, she lifted the smallest sculpture. Though it was only two feet tall, Greer had formed the abstract statue of a man from marble. She felt the weight of it in her hand. Lifted it overhead. She could toss the statue at the Burkes. Or hide beside the door and bring it down on one of them. But what about the other one?

She tried lifting the next size up, an obelisk also made of marble. Though it was slender, she had to slip both hands under it to lift it high enough to do any damage.

She wouldn't have a free hand to hold the other one. She could set the lighter one at her feet where she could grab it immediately after tossing the larger one. She believed that to be the best option.

She carried the heavier sculpture to the door and set it down.

As she returned for the lighter one, voices came through the vent again.

Showtime.

"Remember," Fiona said. "Don't manhandle her. We need to get her out to the cliffs and make it look like her fall was an accident."

"Easier said than done," Greer replied.

"Let me talk to her before you try anything."

"Fine, but if she doesn't cooperate, I'll kill her right here."

"Agreed."

The voices fell silent, and Shannon soon heard the stone moving outside her door. She rushed into position. As the stone's rough surface rubbed against the uneven floor, she felt the vibrations in the wall at her back.

They were coming to end her life, either here in this tiny room or out on the cliff.

Either way, the battle of her life was before her. She hoped she was up to the challenge.

* * *

Michael could barely stand the silence. He'd watched his phone for two hours now. *A watched pot never boils— isn't that how the old saying goes?* The phone refused to ring. He'd tried to keep busy by digging deeper into the Burkes' background but kept hitting dead ends. He periodically tried to connect by phone with someone at the castle but failed. He'd emailed Shannon. He'd followed up with Gavin too. Twice.

So now what?

The phone chimed and he snatched it up, noting "Apple Grove Inn" on the caller ID. "Tom. What have you heard?"

"Betty called. She said there's a big hubbub going on at the castle, and that's why no one answered the phone."

A sense of relief built in Michael's gut, but he wouldn't give it free rein until he heard Shannon was safe. "Everyone's fine, then? Shannon's good?"

"That I'm not quite sure about."

"Not quite? What do you mean?"

"Let me start from the beginning. The police arrived to search Coleen's room. Shannon was with Coleen until the police located the murder weapon—some kind of wine stopper. Then she said something crazy to Coleen about the castle caretakers being art thieves, and she was going to prove it."

"Going where?"

"The cellar, I think. Betty didn't know why the cellar, but then, Shannon does things that don't always make sense."

And they always seemed to put her in danger. "Did you tell Betty to call me?"

"Um, no. You said you wanted to talk to Shannon, so I told her to have Shannon return your call when she gets back."

At the lost opportunity to speak to someone at the castle, Michael wanted to smash his phone against the wall, but it was his only lifeline to Shannon. "Are the police still at the castle?"

"She didn't say."

Of course not. "If Betty or any of the ladies call back, please have them phone me immediately." Michael disconnected and glanced at the clock.

Thirty minutes since he'd last left a message for Gavin. Debriefing or not, Michael dialed him again.

"Michael!" Gavin sounded out of breath. "Sorry about not getting back to you. The meeting took longer than I thought."

"I hope you have good news to report."

"I'm sorry, my friend, but the local authorities have already been to the castle."

"And what did they find?" Michael snapped. "Don't they realize someone is in danger?"

"First of all, we have no proof your friend is in danger. Secondly, two PCs have just returned from the property after executing a search. They said that everything out there is fine. Plus Inspector Watson is still on site in the event that your friend needs his help."

"She's missing. Now! Is this inspector looking for her?"

"That was not mentioned."

Frustration ground at Michael's brain, making his thoughts cloud over. He took a deep breath to gain perspective. This was his best avenue. His only avenue.

His call waiting beeped and he glanced at the phone. Betty. "Hold on, Gavin. Someone is calling from the castle right now."

He clicked over to her call. "Betty, thank goodness you called."

"Tom said you were worried about Shannon, but she still hasn't come back."

"Who talked to her last?"

"Coleen."

"I need to speak to Coleen right now."

"She's behind closed doors with the inspector. They've been there for quite a while now."

Michael stopped pacing and filled his tone with urgency. "Interrupt them."

"What? I can't bust in on the police in a foreign country."

"Have you seen the caretakers? The Burkes?"

"They were here in the grand hall with us until a few minutes ago. They said they had work to do. What's going on, Michael?"

"They're art thieves, and I think they may be the ones who killed Siobhan."

"Impossible."

"It's very possible, and it's also possible Shannon got too close to them and they've abducted her. Coleen is the only one who knows where she went."

"Oh my."

"Move, Betty. Now!" he shouted. "Go to Coleen."

"The signal's bound to drop off."

"If it does, call me back on the castle landline."

"OK, I'm going."

Michael heard her footsteps clipping across the floor until the phone call dropped. He couldn't stand still, so he resumed pacing. He halfheartedly noted locals going about their business on Apple Grove's Main Street, completely oblivious to Shannon's predicament.

"*Possible* predicament," he reminded himself.

His phone soon pealed, and as he answered, he spotted Gavin still on the line. Michael had forgotten all about him.

"Michael." Coleen's Scottish brogue filled the phone. "Shannon went to the cellar."

"Is the inspector still with you?"

"Aye."

"Put him on the phone."

"But—"

"Now!" Michael barked.

"Fine, but I'm listening in." She pressed the phone's speaker button.

"Inspector Watson," the gravelly voice said.

Michael briefly introduced himself. He noted that he was a former police officer in hopes that Watson would feel more inclined to believe the outrageous story he was about to tell. He quickly described the problem. "I have Inspector Gavin Brown, a friend of mine, on hold if you need to confirm I'm not crazy."

"The Burkes have been nothing but cooperative in the investigation."

"Look," Michael said. "What harm would it do for you to go down to the cellar to look for Shannon? It will only take a few minutes, and you could be saving her life."

"*I'll* go," Coleen's voice came over the phone.

"And take off before I can arrest you?" Watson exclaimed. "I'd no more allow that than I'd leave you here alone."

"Take her with you," Michael suggested.

"That would be highly irregular."

"Let's talk, one cop to another. I will do whatever it

takes to make sure Shannon is safe. If that means I have to go above your head, even if I don't want to, I'll do so."

"Fine," Watson grumbled.

"Will you phone me back at this number once you've checked?"

"Aye."

The line went dead and Michael clicked over to Gavin. "I'm sorry that took so long. I spoke to the inspector at the castle. He's going to the cellar to check on Shannon."

"That's good news, then, isn't it?"

"Sure," Michael said. "*If* he finds Shannon alive and well."

*   *   *

The key twisted in the lock and the deadbolt clicked back. Shannon hefted the obelisk above her head and held her breath as the door opened. Time seemed to stand still as she waited for one of the Burkes to step into the room. Nothing happened.

"Put the sculpture down, Shannon," Greer said from outside the door. "I can see the empty pedestals, so I know you have them."

Shannon let go of the breath she held but didn't move.

"Greer has a gun," Fiona warned. "If you try anything, he'll simply shoot you."

Now what should she do?

Think, Shannon, think.

"If you do as he says, we'll let you leave the room."

Yeah, but you'll kill me anyway.

"Shannon," Fiona said. "Please don't make him shoot you. We can work this out."

"Hah," Shannon let slip and instantly wished she hadn't. So what? They knew where she was and what she had in her hands—so what difference did it make?

"Come on, let's talk this through," Greer added, but not very convincingly. "We can come to an agreement that benefits all of us."

"I hope you're not waiting for someone to rescue you." Fiona's tone was growing irritated. "Even if anyone knew where you were, we have the keys you took for the cellar, and Cook is the only other person with a key. She won't hand it over to anyone without an official reason."

Shannon's thoughts drifted to Michael, who'd always been there for her when she'd found herself in dire straits during one of her escapades.

Well, he's not coming for you now, she thought. *He's at home in Apple Grove and oblivious to your predicament.* So maybe she needed to think like him.

What would he do in this situation? Would he take his chances by rounding the corner when Greer had a gun?

No. Michael had seen firsthand the damage a gun could do. He'd surrender and hope that he'd find an opportunity to escape as the Burkes escorted him to the cliff.

"Fine, I'll put it back." Tossing up a prayer for help, she stepped out into the open.

Greer stood outside the door, a pistol clasped in his hands. "Nice and slow now."

"I'm putting it away, like you said." Keeping her focus on Greer, she backed to the pedestal and set down the obelisk.

Greer jerked his gun to the side. "Get the other one. Slowly now."

She retrieved the lighter sculpture and settled it in place. "Now what?"

"Hands up and step to the wall."

She lifted her arms and moved at a snail's pace to the side of the room as directed.

"Tie her hands, Fi," he said to his wife, "and gag her too."

"I know you're taking me to the cliff to make my death look like an accident," Shannon said. "If you tie my hands or gag me, I'll struggle, and it will leave burns and bruises. The police will know it was no accident."

"What do you want me to do?" Fiona asked Greer.

"She has a good point," he said. "We'll have to take her this way."

"But she's a loose cannon."

"We have no choice." He glared at Shannon like it was her fault that he had to kill her. He eased into the room and made his way along the other wall. When he was directly across from her, he slowly approached, one foot in front of the other like a silent panther stalking its prey.

Every instinct in her body said to flee, but her common sense warned her to wait him out. He'd proved he hadn't fully thought through the situation, and the next time he made a mistake, she'd free herself or die trying.

— 21 —

The gun's cold steel pressed at the base of Shannon's skull, reminding her with each step that she could die. Confusion as to their destination warred with her fear. Greer had directed her deeper into the cellar when she'd expected him to whisk her out the tunnel and force her to climb the cliff, only to be hurled from the top.

He pressed the gun deeper. "Faster."

"Not so harsh," Fiona pleaded. "It's bad enough she has to die, but I'd like to think we were kind to her in her last few moments."

Shannon snorted. *I'm going to kill you, but I'll be nice about it.* What kind of logic was that? Absurd for sure. But maybe it meant Shannon could reason with Fiona.

"You can still let me go. I won't tell anyone."

"Hah!" Greer said. "Like we can believe you."

"You believe me, don't you, Fiona?"

"I—"

"Shh," Greer warned. "Someone's coming."

Shannon heard faint footsteps on the stairs.

"Hurry up, Fi. Get that door open now."

Fiona rushed ahead of them and jerked open a door built to look like part of the wall. Greer shoved Shannon through the door and into another hidden stairwell. Fiona dragged the door closed behind them.

"We'll wait here until we're sure no one will hear us."

"Shannon," Coleen's voice came from a distance. "Are you down here?"

Greer painfully buried the barrel in Shannon's neck. "Not a peep out of you."

Would he actually shoot her if she cried out for help?

She couldn't risk it.

She heard a male voice that sounded like Watson tossing out questions to Coleen, but Shannon couldn't make out his words.

"The inspector," Fiona whispered.

"I told you it was worth the time to close up and roll the stone in front of the storage room before we took off," Greer whispered back. "After we dispose of her, we can circle back and grab the paintings." He kept the gun in place and clutched her elbow, urging her to start up the stairs. "Quiet as a church mouse, lovey."

She moved again as slowly as she thought she dared and considered losing her footing to make a sound. But the walls were thick, and it would take a huge commotion to lead Coleen to her.

After winding up one flight of steep stairs, Fiona pressed open a door that led to the castle gardens, bare and forlorn in the winter's air. Cold rushed in with a lash of rain. It took only moments for Shannon's chill to return and her teeth to start chattering. Greer forced her out into the garden. The cold seeped into her feet, and she moved clumsily.

"Pick up the pace, sister." He started moving more quickly, nearly dragging her along.

She kept scanning the area, looking for a way out, to escape, but nothing became clear until she stumbled and nearly fell to the ground. Greer jerked her up, losing his footing in the process.

Fiona quickly came up beside him and righted him, but for a moment, the cold bite of the gun had disappeared and Shannon could've overpowered him if she hadn't been taken by surprise. She needed a chance to take *him* by surprise instead.

Nearing the edge of the garden, she saw her last chance before they broke into the clearing by the cliff. If she timed things perfectly, she might be able to get the best of both the Burkes in one move.

Step by step, they headed toward a thick stand of trees running the length of the garden.

At the last moment before stepping into the clearing, Shannon shifted her hip, barreling it into Greer. He lost his balance, his gun arm jerking up and away from Shannon. She darted into the stand of trees. She hoped Greer had tumbled into Fiona and the pair had fallen to the ground, but Shannon didn't waste time looking back.

She ran, hard and fast. Over decomposing leaves. Over tree roots. Faster and faster. Her frozen feet couldn't feel the ground any longer. Footsteps echoed behind her, but she kept going, darting from tree to tree for safety.

Nearing the castle, her foot caught on a massive tree root and she tumbled to the ground. Her head crashed into the tree trunk. Shaking her head, she tried to clear the dizzying spin and pain as she regained her uncooperative feet. She stumbled like someone on a drinking binge.

"Stop!" Greer called out. "Stop or I'll shoot!"

Shannon doubted he'd risk firing so close to the castle,

so she ignored him. Wobbly and woozy, she moved on. As she caught her foot on another root and tipped to the side, a shot rang out and the bullet whizzed overhead, splintering the tree.

Shocked, she looked back. Anger—red and hot—blazed from Greer's eyes. His face was contorted in rage, and she didn't recognize him as the kindly man who'd been so helpful.

"Don't move, or I'll fire again," he hissed.

"Don't," Fiona said. "We're too close to the castle. Watson will hear if he hasn't already."

Shannon agreed with her logic. She ducked behind the nearest tree and began to shout. "Help! He's trying to kill me! Help!"

"We have to get out of here!" Fiona screamed at Greer. "Now!"

Shannon heard movement, but she didn't stop yelling long enough to see if they were coming toward her or running away.

"Shannon!" Coleen's high-pitched voice came from the other side of the copse of trees.

Shannon sagged with relief before she realized Greer might shoot Coleen too. She cupped her hands around her mouth and yelled, "It's Greer! He has a gun! Don't come in here!"

Coleen didn't reply, and after what felt like an eternity of nothing but the rain beating against her face, Shannon peeked around the tree. Greer and Fiona were gone. She was safe.

She tried to head toward Coleen's voice, but her leg muscles had seized up in the cold, and she couldn't move. She wrapped her arms around her stomach and slid slowly down the tree, curling into a ball to conserve whatever warmth her body still retained. Despite the cold, despite the fear, despite the memory of the whole ugly event, she closed her eyes and rested.

She heard voices, but they sounded like they were coming from a deep tunnel. She blinked several times, gently at first, but then more firmly to clear her vision.

"She's by the tree!" Coleen screamed. "She's alive!" She ran to Shannon and sank to her knees. Tears streamed down Coleen's reddened cheeks. "Don't ever scare me like that again! Do you hear me?"

"You're yelling in my face, so of course I hear you." Shannon smiled.

"Can you stand?"

Shannon nodded, but the dizziness from her fall overpowered her. "The Burkes," she mumbled. "They're art thieves. They killed Siobhan."

"We know." Coleen held up her phone. "Michael told us all about them."

"Michael?" Shannon slowly came to her feet.

"I've been on the phone with him for the last hour. The highlights are ..." Coleen held up her index finger. "One, Michael figured out the Burkes were art thieves." She flipped up another finger. "Two, he tried to get ahold of you via cell, email, the castle phone, and calling every one of the Purls multiple times. Then he called the police. Then he forced Betty to interrupt my interrogation and convinced Watson—who you know is very hard to convince of *anything*—to come looking for you." She lifted the next finger. "Three, even with an ocean separating you, he didn't give up when he thought you were in trouble, and he saved your life."

"I need to thank him," Shannon said earnestly as a gust of wind knocked into her and she shivered.

"We can call Michael after I get you inside and in front of a roaring fireplace." Coleen tucked her free hand under Shannon's elbow.

"We can't hike all the way up the hill in this weather to call him." Shannon slowly moved her feet testing them.

"We can use the castle phone. After what we've been through, I figure the owners of the castle owe us one or two international calls." She looked at Shannon and winked. "And maybe a discount or two on the wedding."

* * *

In a dress of pale blue, Shannon stood before the Purls and Coleen as they waited in the alcove for Coleen's nephew to escort her into the intimate church. Shannon opened the small box she'd brought with her from Oregon and pulled out the top handkerchief where she'd embroidered the bride and groom's names next to the date along with a small replica of the castle's facade.

She handed it to Coleen. "This is going to be a very special, yet emotional, day for all of us. I made one of these for each of us. Not only for practicality, as we'll all be crying tears of joy, but also a keepsake of this amazing trip we've all taken together."

"Och, it's beautiful," Coleen said, tears already forming.

"Hey now, don't start yet," Shannon warned. "At least

get down the aisle before you destroy the hours of work we put into your makeup."

Coleen laughed as she hugged Shannon. "What would I do without you here?"

"You'll never have to find out. I'll always be here for you." A flashback to yesterday's narrow escape popped into Shannon's brain, but she just as quickly laid it to rest. Nothing was going to ruin this special day.

Melanie took out her camera. "Let's get a group picture before the ceremony starts."

The ladies sat on an ornately carved bench, and Coleen's nephew shot the photograph.

When he'd taken a picture Melanie approved of, he turned to Coleen. "It's time for me to escort you now."

"Already?"

He nodded. "Gemma's on her way down from her room."

"We'd better get in there then," Joyce said.

Coleen grabbed Shannon's arm. "Remember, you're sitting in the front pew with me, Ewan, and his mum."

"How could I forget?" Shannon joked. "You've mentioned it at least a thousand times today."

"Och." Coleen swatted at her. "Be gone with you now."

Smiling, Shannon and the Purls strolled down the short aisle with their usher. Shannon took in the small space that seated only one hundred people comfortably. The aisle separated wrought iron-and-wooden pews. Simple white roses cascaded on greenery hung from brass wall sconces. Large arrangements of the same roses sat on antique stands on either side of the small altar, which was housed in an alcove with a rounded stained glass window.

The usher stopped by the pew reserved for the Purls, then escorted Shannon to the front. She sat next to Ewan's mother and wished her well. The groom and best man entered from a side room and stood stiffly in the front. The four-piece string quartet off to the side started playing a classical piece, which meant Coleen was on her way down the aisle. She soon settled in next to Shannon. Coleen rested her hand on her knee and it trembled.

Shannon laid her hand over her friend's to still the tremor. There was a pause as the quartet changed music sheets. Then Pachelbel's *Canon in D Major* floated lightly on the air. Coleen jumped to her feet, and Shannon followed suit. Olivia, stunning in a deep navy gown, made her way down the aisle. Coleen blew her daughter a kiss and then grabbed Shannon's hand when Ewan and Gemma came into view.

Ewan looked distinguished in his black tuxedo, and his usually unruly black hair was subdued with as much gel as he would allow Coleen to mix in before he bolted from the chair.

But, just as Shannon had predicted, Gemma stole the show with her haute couture gown, beaded so expertly by the Purls of Hope. The gasps of awe by everyone proved it.

The silk glided over the rich burgundy runner on wood floors as she moved, and the Swarovski crystals caught and held the lights, looking like a million sparkling diamonds. Coleen, openly crying now, pulled the handkerchief from her sleeve and dabbed her face. Gemma stopped by her mother. "I love you, Mum."

"I love you too," Coleen said as she squeezed Gemma's hand.

Coleen cried through the ceremony, which went off without a hitch. Soon Mr. and Mrs. Sean Hurst turned and greeted their guests. A jovial round of applause broke out, and Coleen turned to Shannon. "I wish you had another one of these lovely hankies. I've used this one up, and the day is only beginning."

Shannon opened her clutch and pulled out a fresh one, then handed it to Coleen. "There are three more in here."

"Och, you know me well, don't you?" Coleen said. "I'll be sure to return the same favor at your wedding."

Shannon rolled her eyes. She had known Coleen would mention Michael at least once today, but Shannon didn't care. With a heart full of joy, she could cut her meddlesome friend some slack on her daughter's wedding day. She was just glad to be here, surrounded by her friends and love, secure in the knowledge that she'd helped put two murderers behind bars where they belonged.

— Epilogue —

Sunday morning dawned bright, the sun beaming down on Shannon as she sat quietly by John's grave while the Purls waited in the van for the drive to the airport. They'd offered to hold her hand and support her through the visit, but a feeling of peace descended on her when they arrived at the cemetery, and she didn't need support.

She lifted her face to the sun's warmth, amazed at how the weather reflected her feelings about John.

"The twins miss you … I miss you," she said to him as she laid a colorful bouquet on the neatly manicured lawn. "You know I will always love you, but I've come out the other side of my grief, and so have the kids. You'll be happy to hear that I'm once again whole. That's what you'd want, isn't it? I'll always cherish our love and the time we had together. The memories we made."

She pressed her hand on his stone, the coolness reminding her of their first encounter. "Remember how we met? That chilly autumn day on campus, when I dropped my books, and you came to my rescue? It was love at first sight, and it lasted for so many years."

Shannon paused. She took a deep breath before continuing.

"There's someone I want to tell you about. I *need* to tell you about. His name is Michael …."

As she talked, visions of how Michael had come into her life to protect her from an unseen foe who wanted to steal her inheritance played like a video in front of her eyes. "It's not the same at all with Michael. We didn't have that instant chemistry like you and me. But that's no surprise. My heart totally belonged to you when I met Michael. Now …." she paused again to search her feelings before speaking them aloud.

A bright yellow bird swooped down from a tall tree and flitted past, drawing her attention for a moment. "Now I think I'm ready to fly again, to live life to the fullest."

Shannon heard the van door slam and footsteps approach.

"Shannon," Coleen whispered as she laid a gentle hand on Shannon's shoulder. "It's time to go."

Shannon stood and brushed grass from her pants. She touched John's stone again. "Goodbye, my love," she whispered as tears formed in her eyes. Deep breaths barely warded them away.

"Ready?" Coleen asked.

Shannon nodded, but she couldn't speak without tears. Coleen took her arm and they strolled toward the van. The same bird looped in front of her, reminding Shannon of her promise to move on.

"Are you OK?"

Shannon felt Coleen watching her, but she followed the bird's progress as it soared toward the top of a tree. Her heart flooded with gratitude for her life. For all that she had. For all she could still experience. She was not only OK—she was wonderful.

"I'm great," she said.

"Did John help you sort out your feelings for Michael?"

Shannon shot a surprised look at Coleen.

"What? I know you better than anyone else. Is it a surprise that I figured out what you talked about?"

"I guess not."

"Then let's get on the road, and you can tell me all about it."

Shannon laughed as she gave her friend a hug. "I don't know what I'd do without you, Coleen Douglas. I'm going to miss you when I get back to Oregon."

"I'm going to miss you too. But you never know—I might have to return to Oregon sooner than either of us thought."

"Oh? Are you hoping we'll stumble upon another mystery?"

Coleen shrugged. "That would be an added bonus. Icing on the cake, if you will. Or perhaps I should say, wedding cake."

"Huh?"

"You know I wouldn't dream of missing my best friend's wedding." Coleen winked.

"Oh, Coleen." Shannon chuckled and shook her head. "You are incorrigible."

Learn more about Annie's fiction books at

AnniesFiction.com

- Access your e-books
- Discover exciting new series
- Read sample chapters
- Watch video book trailers
- Share your feedback

We've designed the Annie's Fiction website especially for you!

Plus, manage your account online!

- Check your account status
- Make payments online
- Update your address

Visit us at AnniesFiction.com

Turn the page for an exclusive preview
of the next mystery in the
Creative Woman Mysteries series.

Murder in Two Acts

COMING SOON!

— 1 —

"**I** wonder who's going to die tonight?" Shannon McClain flashed a mischievous grin at the ladies seated at the table around her.

"Not Essie, I hope. I'd hate to spend all this money just to see her kick the bucket in the first five minutes." Joyce Buchanan chuckled and took a sip of her water. Her bright pink fingernail polish and fuchsia lipstick seemed like a direct contrast to the otherwise drab decorations gracing the dining area of the *Good Times*, a small dinner cruise ship based out of Apple Grove, Oregon.

Dull wood paneling covered the walls, framed but outdated prints hung every several feet, and dusty artificial flowers bloomed in various locations around the perimeter. Yellow, cracked linoleum met their feet.

Huge windows along two walls usually displayed the Pacific Ocean, except right now, night had fallen, and all one could see was inky darkness. Shannon planned on stepping onto the deck during intermission to check out the night-time view and absorb the salty sea air for a moment. She relished the fact that Apple Grove was in such close proximity to both the ocean and the mountains.

Shannon turned her attention back to her friends, who'd all gathered for a Thursday night full of mystery aboard the ship. They were members of a group known as the Purls of Hope. The ladies met weekly to craft together but never missed an opportunity to chat at other times. These women meant the world to Shannon.

"Have any of you ever been to a mystery dinner theater before?" Shannon asked, her voice soft as if she were developing conspiracy theories. She glanced at each person at the table and grinned. "I have to admit this is a first for me."

Joyce, Betty, Melanie, and Kate all shook their heads.

"I've heard about them, and they sound like a hoot," Kate Ellis offered. She nodded her head, her brown ponytail bobbing with the action. Kate, in her early thirties, could pull off the casual look with the best of them. The understated style fit her, especially since she spent most of her days either grooming or pet-sitting various four-legged creatures as part of her business, Ultimutt Grooming.

Shannon looked at the people milling around on the cruise ship. There was a woman wearing a cardigan and pearls, someone carrying a political campaign sign, a man in a football uniform, and nearly a hundred other people, most of whom were sitting at little circular tables.

"If they offer a prize for the person who correctly guesses who the killer is, I know who will get it." Joyce stared at Shannon, eyebrows raised. Her platinum-blond hair, cut in a chic bob, swished as she leaned forward.

"Now, now." Shannon put her water down and waved a hand in the air. "Just because I've cracked a few real-life crimes doesn't mean I'll be able to solve the murder drama here tonight." Her Scottish accent lilted with each word.

Melanie Burkhart pushed her glasses higher on her nose before picking up the playbill for *Class Reunions Can Be Murder* and using it to fan her face for a moment. Melanie, a cancer survivor, worked part time for Shannon and part time as a designer at The Flower Pot florist. She had wavy black hair, glasses, and was in her late forties. The whole place felt like the air conditioning needed to be cranked up a few notches.

"I've always wanted to come to one of these plays," Melanie said. "I'm so excited Essie's a part of it. She's going to do great."

"You're right. I know she'll be wonderful. She excels at anything creative." Shannon should know. Essie Engleman worked at the Paisley Craft Market & Artist Lofts, the business Shannon had inherited from her grandmother, Victoria Paisley. Shannon daily saw Essie's work firsthand, and her creations never failed to amaze her.

"What role did she say she was playing again?" Betty Russo asked. Betty was in her mid-fifties, tall and slender, and she had auburn hair that curled around her face. She was one of the sweetest women Shannon knew.

Shannon smiled when she saw her friend's knitting needles peeking from below the table. Betty never seemed to miss an opportunity to craft. By day, she and her husband, Tom, ran The Apple Grove Inn.

"I'm pretty sure she plays an eccentric artist," Melanie said. She stopped fanning herself long enough to flip the book open and check the listing.

"Oh, she's not typecast, now is she?" Joyce laughed, slapping her hands on the table. Joyce was the boisterous one of the group. Shannon often joined her, never one afraid to make a scene. They should get along fine at the production this evening, given that they both loved interacting with others.

Shannon pushed a lock of curly red hair behind her ear and leaned closer. "Now, Essie warned me that some cast members are not as obvious. They'll be mingling with us as we're eating. She said don't be surprised if someone starts talking about murder."

Another couple sat at their table, filling the remaining two seats. The man wore an expensive suit, complemented with gold cufflinks and designer glasses. The woman wore a leopard-print shirt and carried a name-brand handbag—one that Shannon knew cost hundreds of dollars. Her exotic perfume smelled expensive, its sultry fragrance wafting around the table.

Shannon raised an eyebrow. With the over-the-top screaming of "rich," perhaps the couple was part of the show, as Essie had warned.

"I'm Delaney Lyons," the woman murmured as the man gently helped her with her chair before taking a seat himself.

The man, obviously Delaney's husband, glanced at Shannon and the Purls with something close to disdain in his eyes. He frowned. "I'm Markus."

Introductions went around the table. The seats around them were now full, and more and more people continued to pour onto the *Good Times*. The ship's owner was a brilliant man for renting out the space in order to let the murder mystery dinner theaters be hosted here. The plays provided a great attraction, not only for tourists but also for locals looking for weekend entertainment.

Class Reunions Can Be Murder promised to be a good break from the grind of everyday life, not to mention the mysteries that always seemed to find their way to Shannon, one way or another.

The lights flickered, and everyone quieted down as the production began. Shannon settled back in her chair as a woman wearing a neat cardigan and pearls took the stage. She clapped her hands together and smiled as she tapped the microphone.

"Attention, Class of 1990. We're pleased to have everyone here for our high school reunion. I can never get enough of these events. I love catching up with everyone. I'm Carolyn Andrews, class president, and I was tasked with organizing this event. The festivities will begin in a moment, so until then, soup's on! Or salad's on, I should say. Soup is next." She let out a nervous laugh.

"See? I told you this was going to be a good time." Delaney looked at her husband and raised one finely arched eyebrow. The woman appeared to be in her mid-forties and had stylish red hair cut in a sharp wedge. The way her voice crooned with each word only confirmed to Shannon that she'd either had a privileged upbringing or she was one of the actors.

Markus pursed his lips and subtly raised his chin. He had to be closer to fifty. His graying hair was gelled, and it spiked slightly in the front. The man was probably twenty pounds overweight, but he carried it well, evenly distributed in a way that made him seem solid instead of heavy. "The theater has never been my idea of a good time, darling."

"I'm trying to expand your horizons and open you up to new experiences." His wife fluttered her hand in the air before shaking her head in frustration.

"That's why I married *you*." His words sounded less than sincere.

"I'd hate for you to become a stuffy bore." She took a dainty sip of her water.

Shannon raised her eyebrows, unsure if they were innocently sparring or if there was underlying agitation to their interaction. Either way, Shannon felt like she was eavesdropping and turned back to her friends.

Shannon cleared her throat. "Anyone here ever go to their class reunions?"

Before anyone could answer, Delaney excused herself to go outside for a smoke.

Joyce nodded and raised her hand. "I wouldn't miss them for the world. I simply love seeing everyone. I especially love it when the skinny minnies from high school have gained weight." She chuckled. "Makes me feel better about myself!"

Shannon laughed. Joyce might have a womanly figure, but she was anything but fat. She was beautiful inside and out with her platinum-blond hair and vivacious smile. All her old classmates should watch out. The woman had made a name for herself as one of the best bakers in Oregon. She owned the Pink Sprinkles Bakery in Apple Grove.

"I've never had much desire to see my classmates," Melanie said. "I was never popular. I keep in touch with a few people, and we get together for dinner occasionally. That's enough for me."

Before Betty or Kate could answer, movement caught Shannon's eye. She pointed to the scene unfolding in the corner of the dining room. "Check it out over there."

The football player and politician were having a heated

argument, and their voices rose above the rest of the crowd. They were obviously part of the show, talking loudly so everyone would pay attention.

"I told you not to bring that up." The politician spoke in a loud whisper. "Do you know what that would do to my campaign?"

The football player scoffed. "Look, dude, I don't know why you think you're going to be elected anyway. Who'd want to vote for you? There's something missing. It's called likability."

The politician's face reddened. "I'm way more qualified for the job than that stingy Williamson Adams. He thinks he can win on good looks and charm alone."

"Is anyone ever elected for being smart but offensive?" The football player's retort served as a verbal slap in the face.

The politician raised his voice and stepped closer. "Look here, beefhead, you may have bullied me in high school, but if you think you're going to jerk me around now that we're adults, you're out of your mind!"

"We'll see what's stronger—brains or brawn." The football player leaned toward the other man. "I wouldn't bank on your victory yet, Mr. Red, White, and Blue. If there's one thing I know how to do, it's win. Three state championships while I was at Ridgeside High. Need I remind you?"

The class president wandered by Shannon's table at that moment and loudly whispered, "Need he remind anyone? He probably mutters it in his sleep. He won't let anyone forget. *Ever.*"

Chuckles circulated through the room.

A waitress set salads in front of each person at the

table just as Delaney returned, the smell of cigarette smoke clinging to her.

The politician and the football player disappeared to different sides of the dining area, and Ms. Class President went to another table, where those seated cracked up at something she mumbled to them.

Shannon was enjoying the experience already. It was like a roller coaster; it got a person's adrenaline pumping even though there was no real danger.

"A mystery without any of the real-life repercussions. That sounds great to me." Shannon let out a long, contented sigh.

"When's Essie going to come out?" Kate's head swiveled, searching the room for her friend. "I can't wait to see her in action."

Delaney looked up as she poured a creamy dressing over her leafy green salad. "You have a friend in the production, do you?"

Kate nodded. "That's right. She's an artist through and through, and coincidentally, that's what she's playing in the show tonight. She's been practicing for weeks, but she didn't give us any details. What will her motivation be? We know she'll either be a victim or a suspect. Isn't that what every member of the cast is?"

"Shannon, you should audition. You'd be great," Joyce said.

Shannon shook her head. "I'm not an actress. I was in one play in elementary school, and I froze as soon as I saw the audience. I get terrible stage fright."

"You seem like you'd be a natural," Kate said.

"I'm definitely not a performing artist. I'm the quiet, reclusive kind." Shannon offered a wide grin.

"We all know that's not true!" Joyce said. "Not the quiet part, at least."

"Is that your friend?" Delaney pointed a well-manicured finger across the room.

Just then, Essie emerged through a doorway by the kitchen area. She was dressed as a stereotypical painter, wearing paint-splattered clothes and a beret while carrying an artist's color palette. In her late twenties, Essie was the youngest of their group. Tonight, she'd pulled her long, blond curls into a side ponytail.

Shannon paused with a bite of salad in the air. Was she just acting, or was Essie really upset? Something about her friend seemed wrought with tension. Essie looked around the room, and her eyes narrowed when she saw Class President chatting with Mr. Politician.

Just part of the show, Shannon reminded herself. She let out a nervous laugh and took a bite of her salad, reminding herself this was supposed to be entertaining. Here she was, overthinking something as simple as a play.

Class President flounced back to the front. "By the way, if you'll turn your attention to this painting onstage, we're auctioning it off tonight. You may place your silent bids on this handy-dandy clipboard here on the stage. The painting was done by our very own Lillian Rodgers. I'm sure you all remember her ... or not." She let out a nervous laugh. "She was more of the quiet and brooding type. Some people might have even called her weird, but look at her work now! Isn't it fabulous?"

Essie—playing Lillian—crossed her arms and glared at Class President before wandering closer to Shannon's table.

Still in character, she leaned toward them. "That woman is so stuck on herself. Who does she think she is? Some things never change, not even after high school."

Essie stormed toward Football Player.

"And the plot thickens," Joyce muttered.

Which of these cast members is going to die? Shannon wondered. There was the politician, the football player, the class president, and the artist. There were more cast members, some of whom hadn't even been introduced yet.

As Shannon took her last bite of salad, the waitress returned to collect their plates. Another waitress—a young, slender woman with dark hair streaked with multicolored highlights—came behind her with a tray loaded with steaming bowls of soup.

"Clam chowder," the waitress announced as she slid the bowls in front of the guests at the table. She stopped by Markus. "You have a shellfish allergy, right? We're bringing you a special dish."

He nodded. "Any day I can avoid anaphylactic shock is a good one."

The waitress nodded, unshaken by the man's off-putting demeanor. "I'll have it right out for you. Vegetable beef. I hope that's OK."

"Not my favorite, but it will do. What do you expect from events like these? Nothing first class, that's for sure."

Mr. Politician came to their table and bantered with them, handing out fake election flyers.

As he talked about the woes of high school, Shannon thought back to her own years in Scotland. It seemed like some things were universal, and high school dynamics was one of them. Even in Scotland, there'd been cliques, some full of popular kids, some with jocks, others with more creative types. Shannon had mostly hung out with the artists, but she'd tried to be friends with everyone. After all, people who were different from Shannon were interesting and inspired her creativity even more.

The waitress came out and set a steaming bowl of soup by Markus. He immediately pushed it away and frowned.

"You should at least try a bite," Delaney said. "They did fix it especially for you." She addressed the rest of the table. "Story goes that he discovered his allergy at the most inopportune time. Where else but high school? I didn't know him back then, but I've heard about it at every class reunion."

He scowled at his wife. "That was back before food allergies were all the rage. Nearly died right there on the dance floor at prom after eating some shrimp cocktail." His eyes narrowed further. "Not one of my fondest memories—or a topic for dinner conversation, especially with strangers."

Markus stared at the bowl in front of him for another moment before pulling it toward him. He dipped his spoon into the liquid and looked at his wife, his eyes narrowed. "A bite, just to get you off my case," he muttered.

He brought the broth to his lips, sipped, and then sputtered. *Too hot?*

His sputtering turned into an all-out cough. He stood, pounding the table. His face reddened. His hand went to his stomach.

Delaney jumped to her feet and beat his back.

Suddenly, the man fell onto the floor, totally motionless. Gasps sounded around them, followed by mutters. *Is this real?*

Shannon's thought was probably repeated throughout the room, but when she looked up and saw the tears streaming down Delaney's face, Shannon realized this was not part of the play.

Reaching into her purse, she grabbed her cellphone and dialed 911.